"Well, explain this Internet-dating scheme to me then, 'cos I just plain don't get it."

"You don't have to get it. It has nothing to do with you."

"Doesn't it?"

She swung round so suddenly he walked straight into her and had to reach out his hands to grasp hold of her upper arms to steady them both.

Maggie felt her skin heat where he was touching, felt the warmth moving up her arm and spreading across her chest. Her heart fluttered and she looked up at him from beneath long lashes. Sean looked down at her with his deep, fathomless dark eyes, the smile still on his lips, and her cheeks flushed a deeper red than before.

Swallowing, she took a shaky breath and asked, "How could it possibly have anything to do with you?"

TRISH WYLIE

resides in the border counties between the north and south of Ireland, splitting her not-long-enough days between her horses and her writing. She started writing in primary school and dreamed about writing romances from the moment she first read one in her early teens. She admits that it's important she's a little in love with her heroes. That way she can write what her heroine is feeling with more conviction and keep alive the hope that her own Mr. Right might still be out there!

O'Reilly's Bride

TRISH WYLIE

SILHOUETTE *Romance*®

Published by Silhouette Books

America's Publisher of Contemporary Romance

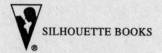 SILHOUETTE BOOKS

ISBN-13: 978-0-373-19837-5
ISBN-10:   0-373-19837-X

O'REILLY'S BRIDE

First North American Publication 2006

Copyright © 2006 by Trish Wylie

Visit Silhouette Books at www.eHarlequin.com

Printed in U.S.A.

Fresh, sparkling and packed with emotion,
Silhouette Romance® brings you a
brand-new book from...

TRISH WYLIE

This new Irish author has a writing style that's
brimming with lyrical warmth and sparky characters.

Next month Harlequin Romance®
brings you Trish's next book,

Project: Parenthood #3922

Teagan Delaney has made sure that she's too busy for
love...too busy to get hurt! But when she has to become
stand-in mom to her sister's tiny kids, and enlists the help
of her gorgeous neighbor Brendan McNamara, the rules
Teagan has lived by begin to crumble....

For Steve & Esther, who got their family.

CHAPTER ONE

'WE'RE just going to have to face up to the fact that we have no choice but to sleep together.'

Maggie watched with widening eyes as Sean launched himself into the air and landed on his side on the huge double bed. After a couple of large bounces, caused more by the weight of his large frame than overly generous springing inside the hotel bed, he rolled onto his side and propped an elbow so he could rest his head on his hand.

He patted the mattress with his free hand. 'Come on over.'

She blinked as he winked at her.

'You know you want to.'

Hell, yes, she wanted to. As the local-TV news team, they'd just spent the last seventeen hours following the police covering the disappearance of a missing twelve-year-old. Thankfully the search had happily ended in the boy being found, cold and hungry, inside the cellar of a derelict house.

Now Maggie was exhausted, her eyes dry and red with lack of sleep. The very idea of a comfy double bed with soft covers and cushions to put her head on was enough to practically draw a low moan from her lips. But the sight of her cameraman's long, lean body lying on it was enough to keep her from the delights of sleep.

There was no way she was going to share a bed with him. Uh-uh. Nope. Just not happening. There was only so far friendship between men and women stretched these days. Well, at least once you'd passed the age of about ten. And Sean was a good twenty years past ten. Twenty-three years, five months and four days if her analytical mind remembered the facts correctly.

With a deep sigh and the folding of her arms across her chest she answered his invitation with a calm voice. 'You can have the sofa. You're used to roughing it. I'm not.'

He grinned. 'I'm too big for that wee sofa. And you wouldn't sleep if you were lying feelin' all guilty about how cramped up I'd be. I know you.'

Her small burst of laughter came out with what she hoped was a graceful snort. 'I'd give it a bloody good try.'

'It's not my fault there was only this room left.'

'No, and it's not my fault that tradition dictates that, as the only man here, you should at least pretend to be gentlemanly.'

'Don't get your corset in a twist, Miss Austen. We live in a modern age of equality now.'

'I am not sleeping in that bed with you.'

'*You're* small enough for the sofa.'

Her green eyes flickered towards the small sofa. It looked plush enough but it *was* tiny. She guessed the usual occupants of this particular room didn't have that great a need for sitting. Sean continued grinning and running his hand back and forth along the duvet cover. 'Seems an awful waste of a honeymoon suite though. Don't you think?'

She laughed, knew she shouldn't have when she saw the answering sparkle in his dark eyes, but laughed anyway. 'A desperate waste altogether.'

'Then the very least we can do is share the bed. The room demands it.' His hand stilled and he fixed her gaze with his darkly sparkling eyes. 'I can manage to control myself if you can.'

Ah, now, but that was just the thing, wasn't it? The knack for flirting with each other, that they'd both got ever so good at, made this situation all the more difficult.

A few months ago, when Sean had been like a child in a toy store where women were concerned, Maggie would have had no problem sharing a bed with him. Because at the time she'd thought he was a friendly version of lice, relationship-wise.

But since she'd moved into the apartment across the hall from him, spent more 'quality' time in his company, got to know him, really know him, they'd become genuine friends. He'd cleaned up his addiction to airheads and the next thing Maggie had known she was batting her eyelashes at him!

So with all the flirting stuff going on and knowing that she genuinely liked him, the last great idea she could have would be sharing a bed with him. In a honeymoon suite, of all places. *And* in an exhaustive state.

Not a good combination for maintaining that fine line between friendship, and, well, other stuff. And she just couldn't focus on any 'other stuff' when she had other 'other stuff' to cope with in her life now. Serious stuff.

'I know it will be hard for you to resist me.'

Her eyes widened again at the low, sexy tones to his voice. Oh, yeah, him using a bedroom voice would help.

'How do you get that head through doors?'

'Well, I'm in here so there must be a way.'

'Amazing.' She shook her head and began to peel off her coat. 'We should do a story on how you manage that.'

His dark eyes watched as the jacket was removed and her shoes were kicked off. She then sat on the edge of the small sofa and unclipped her hair, shaking her head to allow the long auburn curls to frame her face.

Her eyes eventually rose to meet his again. 'You're not going to move, are you?'

He shrugged. 'I might think about it if you continue to undress in front of me. I'd swap a night on the bed for that little show.'

A traitorous giveaway of a beating pulse throbbed in a vein in her neck and Maggie lifted a hand to cover it. She tilted her head a little and rubbed her fingers against the back of her neck to disguise what she was doing.

'I'd even pay money, to be honest.'

'Ooh, now, that would put me in a whole different profession, wouldn't it?'

'Everyone should have the chance to change careers if they want to.'

Her hand stilled and she glanced at him from beneath long lashes. 'Like you did.'

He shrugged. 'I didn't exactly change.'

'Giving up making award-winning documentaries on war-torn countries to filming the local news wasn't much of a change, right enough.'

He grimaced slightly. 'I guess some people would see it as a downgrade.'

'Some people would, but do you, now that you've been at this a while?'

He studied her for several long moments and then smiled a very small smile. 'Some might. I don't. You wouldn't by any chance be trying to change the subject here, would you, Mary Margaret?'

She smiled at the full use of her given name. To everyone else she was just plain old Maggie. But when Sean used her full name it had started out as a way of teasing her. Here, in the provocative surroundings of a honeymoon suite, it was almost an endearment.

'You wouldn't by any chance be trying to avoid having a real conversation by flirting with me, would you, Sean O'Reilly?'

'I might be tempted to open up if you were over here beside me.'

'Might you?'

The question remained in her eyes long after her

words faded into the air and Sean faltered for a moment, his eyes avoiding hers. He blinked as he studied the duvet cover, his hand automatically smoothing it again as he spoke in a low voice. 'Maybe if you trusted me not to molest you in the night I might consider answering some of your questions.'

Maggie studied the dark hair on his head as she thought over the offer. So far their friendship had been limited to everyday conversations and simple truths about family and friends. They'd talked movies and books and current affairs on their many car journeys around the country but nothing deeper than that. Already she knew enough about him to have become attached to him, to care. But what she'd learned so far made her want to know even more why he had made so drastic a change to his life. She felt that knowing that would slot the rest of what she knew into place, would give her the complete picture.

It was almost too good an opportunity to miss.

But she also knew that there had been tension in the air between them lately. A very sexual tension. And the only way she knew of to ease that some and veer away from it was to make him smile. Because she couldn't allow herself to get involved with him on a sexual level, no matter how much her body reacted to the idea. Not while a cloud hung over her.

'OK. I'll just have to trust you to be good.'

The required smile was instantaneous as he looked back at her and winked. 'Honey, I'm way more than good.'

Maggie rolled her eyes. 'I'll take your word for that.'

'You could find out.'

'No, I couldn't.' She stood up and began to walk towards the bathroom, her chin held high. 'Because nothing is going to happen. I'm going to trust you.' At the door of the bathroom she looked back over her shoulder and smiled sweetly. 'And I'm going to ask you personal questions till you're so tired you'll snore the rest of the night away.'

Sean watched the door close behind her and continued to smile until her words sank in. It was a big step for him. Huge, in fact. Because he hadn't talked to anyone about his reasons for coming home. He hadn't met anyone whom he thought could take listening to it.

Could Mary Margaret Sullivan? Could she listen to all the horrors and understand? He needed to talk about it to someone so that he could start to put it behind him. And he guessed he'd known for a while that she was a candidate for a listening ear. It had just been much easier to hide behind flirting with her.

Spending the night convincing her of how 'good' he could be was certainly a more inviting prospect.

But maybe it was time he allowed himself to make a genuine friend, one who *really* knew him. He may not tell her everything in one go, but hey, it would be a start.

She reappeared from the bathroom ten minutes later. At the sound of the door opening he turned on the bed and his breath caught. It wasn't going to be easy baring his soul in a gigantic queen-size bed with a woman who looked like *that*. He could think of much better things to do. Lots of them, in fact.

It wasn't that she'd dressed to seduce him. Oh, no, nothing that simple from Mary Margaret. In fact, he guessed she probably looked that way every night when she went to bed. All freshly scrubbed face and a simple two-piece pyjama suit in a baby pink. There was nothing vaguely sexual in the way she looked. It was the fact that she looked so sweet and fresh, so untouched by the sordid things of the world.

For the first time in his world-weary life he was immediately and ragingly turned on by pink cotton pyjamas.

'What?'

He blinked and forced himself to look up into her large green eyes. How in heaven's name did she manage to look better without make-up? His sisters had always told him that wasn't humanly possible.

'What?'

When he didn't reply, she shook her head. 'You are a weirdo sometimes, O'Reilly.'

Dark eyes watched as she moved around the end of the huge bed. It was a fairly long walk so he had plenty of time to look. She hesitated when she got to 'her side'.

One dark eyebrow rose. 'There's plenty of room, Mary Margaret.'

Not enough though.

She lifted the cover and got in, keeping as close

to the edge as she could without falling out. She tried closing her eyes, inviting sleep to take her.

'You going to sleep?'

'Yes.'

'No bedtime story?'

'Oh, I'm listening. You can start any time.'

Sean moved over, lying on his side with his head propped on his elbow so he could study her face. He smiled as her mouth pursed into a thin line, then her nose wrinkled and she sighed, 'What's wrong?'

'When we got here I was wiped. Now I can't sleep.'

He was still smiling when her eyes opened.

She smiled back, then turned to face him across the huge divide. 'So talk to me.'

'What do you want to know?'

The thought of actually getting to ask whatever she wanted made her even more awake than she already was from the way he'd looked at her when she came out of the bathroom. His eyes had positively burned her from the huge bed he was occupying. And the sight of his broad naked chest above the covers had woken her up pretty quick.

Trying hard to ignore the sight of that chest within an arm and a half's reach, she tried to decide what to ask first. 'How can you be happy doing what you're doing now?'

'Maybe it's the company I keep.'

She blinked at him with large eyes.

He smiled a smaller smile and let his eyes rove up to her hair, the faint smell of her shampoo making it all the way across to him. He liked that smell. Then his eyes met hers again. 'It's simpler, less soul-destroying. I guess I just needed this right now.'

Maggie stared deep into his eyes, searching. Searching for evidence that he was being honest when her heart already told her he was.

'Something to make you smile again, huh?' Her voice was low, all the more intimate in their present surroundings. 'You didn't smile a whole lot when I first met you.'

'No, I guess I didn't.' His voice dropped to a similarly intimate level. 'Maybe you just brought that out in me.'

She was being sucked in by the moment. Any second she fully expected there to be violins in the background and they would move across the great divide and—

She shook her head.

He laughed. 'What?'

'It's just nice to know that when you looked through that lens the sight you saw was so amusing. I'm flattered.' She smiled a small smile to let him know she was teasing.

'You had your moments.'

Her mind turned for a small moment, then she propped her elbow and raised her hand so she could lift her head and rest it there. 'So is it enough for you?'

'Looking at you through a lens every day?' He managed to hold his smile even as he realised it was precisely enough for him. He loved looking at her.

Had been doing more and more of it recently, and not just through a lens. Had she noticed that he'd stopped dating recently? Because he was only just discovering why it was he'd stopped.

'You can quit that, I know what you're doing.'

'I thought I was flirting with you.'

'You are. But you're only doing it to distract me.'

'Is it working?'

Yes. 'No.'

'Damn.'

She laughed and watched as his eyes sparkled in response. 'Tell me something else.'

'You're the reporter, you ask the questions.'

'Will you stay?' Her breath caught when she spoke the question aloud as soon as it entered her head. It was something she really needed to know. 'Or is this just a break for you?'

Dark lashes brushed against his skin once, twice, as he blinked at her. 'I'm not going back there, if that's what you mean.'

'Never?'

'Never again.' He shook his head. 'I guess you could say I'm burned out when it comes to overseas work. I want to make a life here now. I just needed to come home, that's all.'

'Does it help?'

His nod was slow. 'It does now that I have this new friend.'

The answering smile was warm and sincere. 'I'm glad.'

Sean watched as she set her head back down on

the pillow, her eyes closing again. 'You want to sleep now?'

'I think I have to, I'm sorry.' Her eyes flickered open and she glanced up at him. 'I've still a lot to ask, though.'

'We have time, Mary Margaret, don't worry.' His eyes glowed across at her in the soft light. 'Sweet dreams.'

CHAPTER TWO

SOMETHING changed.

Sean couldn't narrow it down to a precise moment in time or some circumstance in particular. But something changed. And the fact that it changed around the time he was finally admitting he had a thing for Maggie didn't help his inner turmoil any.

She was *hiding* something from him.

The first thing he'd noticed was how she would turn her eyes away from him. It was one of the things he'd always liked about her. She would look a person straight in the eye when she talked to them, would let them know they had her full attention. And it was a great trait for a reporter. People trusted that she was listening, that what they said mattered to her.

But now she would look down, her lashes hiding the windows to her soul when she spoke to him. And sometimes she even seemed to struggle to look him directly in the lens. Probably because she knew he might see something there.

Then there was the sadness. Not that she didn't hide that pretty well. Every day she would smile, crack jokes with her workmates, laugh. But as a connouiseur of her laughter he knew that even that was missing something. It took a lot of careful scrutiny for him to spot the sadness, but it was there. In the unguarded moments when she thought no one was looking or for a split-second before she turned her eyes away.

Something had changed.

When she jumped the day that he crept up behind her in the office he smelt a rat. She was quick to flick the screen of her computer off before she fobbed him off with something about his not having yelled 'boo' and how she had been writing a personal e-mail. But that was a lie, Sean knew, because she looked away as she said it and she had been jumpy as all hell for the rest of the day.

It took a lot of investigative work for him to get to the bottom of it. But he got there. Eventually.

And when he did he couldn't have been more knocked sidewards.

With determined steps he walked across the lawn of the big old country manor that had been turned into luxury apartments. Apartments where he and Maggie lived.

It was a gorgeous summer's day and a great place for a birthday barbeque for one of their neighbours. But Sean wasn't thinking about the celebrations. Or the food. Or even the beer clutched in his hand.

He was thinking about Maggie. And her latest brainwave.

'Fancy meeting you here.'

He grinned, immediately recognising her smile for what it was. A front specifically for his benefit.

'Yeah, fancy that.' He took a swig of beer and stood by her side, his feet set slightly apart, claiming the piece of ground he was standing on while he looked at the small crowd and glanced occasionally at Maggie from the corner of his eye. 'Don seems to be having a good time.'

Maggie looked over at their neighbour. 'Yeah, he does.' With a safe topic to discuss she immediately slipped into the easy role that until a few months ago had been so natural to her, leaning a little closer to Sean and nudging her shoulder against his upper arm. 'You see the way he keeps looking at Rachel?'

Sean leaned his head a little closer to hers and dropped his voice conspiratorially. 'She keeps looking at him too, when she thinks he can't see her.'

The subject of the octogenarian love affair was one they frequently talked about. Maggie smiled and tilted her head to look up into dark eyes, her voice low. 'You think they'll ever get it together? Or is that still too much of a stretch for you into the realms of believing good things *can* happen?'

Sean's eyes locked with hers and he stared at her for a long moment. 'I'm learning to stretch some. So, maybe it might happen yet. They've been friends a long time though.'

'Yes, they have, but you only have to see the way they are together to know there's more there.'

He blinked slowly and smiled.

Maggie searched his eyes, looking from one to the other. She tilted her head to the other side and searched again, then an eyebrow quirked and she asked, 'What?'

The smile remained. 'What?'

She stared back at him. 'You have a look.'

'Do I?' He continued smiling his usual self-assured smile, his eyes giving nothing away.

It bugged the hell out of Maggie that he had the ability to do that and that he still felt the need to do it around her. He was just so controlled sometimes that she wanted to smack him silly. He held everything inside, guarded from the world so that in the brief instances he did open up it made it all the more of a gift to whoever was allowed in. But he still didn't completely trust her, did he?

The fact that she'd had to hold back so much from him of late made the realisation almost hurtful. She hated that a relationship that had come to mean so much to her had got to this point.

He searched her eyes in a similar way to how she'd just searched his. 'What?'

She mimicked his answer. 'What?'

'That mind of yours works in mysterious ways.'

'At least I have a mind.'

'Meaning I don't?'

She only had to search for the briefest of seconds to find the spark in his eyes. 'Not you, but possibly some of those other women you keep company with…'

'At least they have brains enough to see what an amazingly sexy, damned good-looking, generally all-round great guy I am.'

What would usually have been taken as one of their usual 'sparring type' answers was imparted with a somewhat huskier tone of voice than Maggie was used to hearing from him. But as she searched his eyes again he turned his head and looked back over the crowd, raising his bottle to his mouth.

Maggie's eyes automatically followed the bottle, watched as his mouth fitted around the lip, saw his throat contract as he swallowed. She hated that she noticed but she did.

'I already know what a great guy you are.' The words were spoken with sincerity, even though she didn't have to point out that she hadn't agreed with the other descriptions of his 'assets'.

'Do you, now?' He studied the last of the liquid in the bottle, swirling it around against tinted glass.

Maggie felt her heart miss a beat at his question. He had an uncertainty in him she'd never seen before. Sean was just always so confident on the outside. Everything he did, the way he held himself, it all spoke of a complete lack of self-consciousness. Until now. What *had* her sister said to him during the long conversation they'd been having on the far side of the lawn?

'OK, what's going on?'

He didn't look at her. 'You're the one who seems to think that any woman interested in me might not have a brain in their head.'

Maggie frowned. 'I was kidding.'

'Were you?' He glanced at her, then away again.

The question astounded her. For crying out loud she had even introduced him to a couple of the women he had dated way back at the start. That was, until she'd learned better than to get involved in all that would inevitably follow. Now she guarded her single friends with the ferocity of a lioness guarding innocent cubs.

But those earlier women most certainly had not been brainless. They had been smart, successful, pretty women. Like anyone he had been even remotely interested in. So what was with the sudden concern? It wasn't as if he'd even done that much dating of late. She'd noticed *that*.

The thought then crossed her mind that maybe he had met someone he had more than a passing interest in. She'd certainly been less aware of him being with anyone new but that didn't mean there wasn't somebody. Maybe he was serious about someone and having those feelings was making him insecure. Wasn't that what happened with something that important?

The idea made her stomach churn ridiculously and she had to take a deep breath when she looked away from his profile. God only knew she wanted him to be happy, to learn about real love and to have all the things he hadn't quite completely admitted out loud he wanted for himself down the line. A woman to love, to love him back. A family of his own. Children who would look just like him.

Maggie wanted those things for him.

But that didn't mean that losing something of the friendship and the closeness they had wouldn't hurt. Even the thought of it already hurt. Because in her own way she was already taking the initial steps that would distance her from him.

Clearing her throat, she looked down at the ground

and then back at his profile. 'Did you meet some-one new?'

His eyes shot round to meet hers and he wanted to ask her if it would matter. But the words got stuck. He smiled to ease the tension. 'Me?'

She smiled back at him, her composure in place. 'Yes, you, unlikely and all as that may be. You tend to go through women faster than most.'

'No, I didn't meet someone new.' He said the words softly and watched for her reaction. To see if she looked at all relieved. But when she just contin-ued to smile at him he jumped right on in with both feet. 'But then *I* haven't advertised myself anywhere or felt the need to, funnily enough. Unlike someone I could mention.'

Her smile faltered. So that was it, then. Her sister had told him about that during their little tête-à-tête on the other side of the lawn. She straightened her spine again and moved a couple of steps away from his side.

'I may as well have announced it on the news.'

He continued to study her intently before she turned her face from him. 'What's going on?'

'If you've been talking to Kath then you know exactly what's going on.'

'She said you've decided to hunt down some poor unsuspecting single parent.' His mouth twisted at one edge. 'What's the thinking there, then? You want to make sure he can be a good father before you tie yourself down? Sort of already broken in, kinda thing?'

Maggie flushed under his scrutiny. 'Funny, Sean, really hilarious. You just have such insight into the female mind that it's a miracle you've stayed single this long.'

He frowned at the sharp tone in her voice; frowned even harder when she turned on her heel and walked away. In the space of a heartbeat he was on her heel. 'Well, explain it to me, then, 'cos I just plain don't get it.'

'You don't have to get it. It has nothing to do with you.'

'Doesn't it?'

She swung round so suddenly he walked straight into her and had to reach out his hands to grasp hold of her upper arms to steady them both. A little juggling saved both them and his bottle from an ungraceful contact with the hard ground that would have been aided by a small thing known as gravity.

When they were both firmly on their feet his hands remained, his hold loosening a little, thumbs brushing back and forth against her skin. He laughed. 'Did the earth move for you too?'

Maggie felt her skin heat where he was touching, felt the warmth moving up her arm and spreading across her chest. Her heart fluttered and she looked up at him from beneath long lashes. Sean looked down at her with his deep, fathomless dark eyes, the smile still on his lips, and her cheeks flushed a deeper red than before.

Swallowing, she took a shaky breath and asked,

'How could it possibly have anything to do with you?'

He wondered if she had any idea how much she had got under his skin? They'd been flirting around a deeper involvement up until recently; he wasn't so stupid that he didn't know that. But did it really add up to anything more in Maggie's mind? Or was it simply wishful thinking on his part?

He took the one safe route open to him. 'Can't your best mate worry that you might make a mistake?'

Maggie avoided his eyes while her mind worked on an answer to his question. She'd known he would probably have the most difficulty with what she'd decided to do. That he would push the most to find the motive behind her decision. He cared about her in his own very individual way, she knew that much. Knew it and had to skirt around it for reasons of her own.

She could never tell him the truth. Because if he knew he would try to stop her, would argue every step of the way unless she was very much mistaken. And she'd already made up her mind. There could *be* no shifting her. No turn-around.

His thumbs continued to move against her skin. Soothing, reassuring and letting her know that he was right there, beside her, *with her*. But little did he know that the touch did more than reassure and the last thing it did was soothe.

For months she had been fighting the pull towards him. At first she hadn't wanted to face up to the fact that she could even see him that way. As anything more than just a friend, a buddy, her pal, her mate. But it had just been so strong, so very real that it had scared her. It had been a losing battle though.

Even now, while his thumbs moved back and forth and back and forth, her blood was humming in her veins, her skin was heating, her pulse was beating irrationally. She couldn't let him keep touching her. Bad, bad plan.

Sean watched as she moved out of his hold. He frowned when she seemed to shiver, before wrapping her arms around herself. And she still couldn't look him in the eye.

If she was this disgusted by him touching just her *arms* then he was way off base with what he'd thought had been happening between them.

He frowned harder.

'You don't need to worry about me, Sean. I know what I'm doing.' She smiled with a little more conviction as she forced out the words she had been rehearsing in front of a mirror for days. 'You know how much I want a family; we've talked about it loads. The more the merrier, as far as I'm concerned. I'm sick to death of the whole singles thing and I'm not getting any younger. I don't want to wait till I'm old before I find the right guy.' She paused for a breath. 'I tripped across the site when I was doing some background on the dating scene for that piece we did last month and it just made sense to me. That's all.'

He blinked the whole way through her speech and then asked, 'Is it?'

'Oh, for crying out loud, yes!' The fact that he was still asking questions with that deadpan expression was making her more and more nervous. 'Why does it need to be any more complicated than that? We've talked about what we'd both like from our lives since that night in the honeymoon suite and for me a family is the most important thing. I'm just doing something about it, that's all.'

That was all. And she'd never even considered him in that equation. Why would she? It wasn't as if he'd given the impression it was something he wanted in the here and now. It was only recently he'd even allowed himself to admit inwardly that it *was* something he wanted. How could he have expected her to know? He wasn't exactly an open up and share kind of guy after all. Not with the deep stuff anyway.

'Fine.' He took a breath and looked away from her. 'Good luck with that. Just be sure you don't end up chatting to some speckly faced kid.'

She waited several long moments before she replied. Ignoring the jibe at the end of his sentence, she decided to take the easy route out with a softly spoken, 'Thank you.' And then she walked away.

Sean frowned as he watched her leave. He drained the remnants of his bottle and then marched off in search of a new one.

He'd been very wrong on this thing he had with Maggie, or had thought he had with Maggie. There were no visible signs of her holding an unrequited adoration for him. It was just an awful shame that he didn't feel the same way.

But he wasn't about to spill that to her when she was so obviously uninterested. Because he might have lost his mind but he wasn't about to part with his pride. There were limits.

But he had thought, for a while, that there was something more there for her too. He wasn't an adolescent or so inexperienced that he hadn't noticed when she'd looked at him with a slow-burning smoulder in her eyes. Maybe it had even been the catalyst for his own silent smouldering. But *something* had changed her mind. Something more involved than what she'd just stated was behind this scheme of hers. And even if she wasn't in love with him, the part of him that was her friend, that cared so much, just couldn't stand by and let her make a big mistake. Not if her motives weren't genuine.

He was going to find out what was going on. Whether she liked it or not. Because it mattered to him. He might not be able to show how much he cared right that minute but he could show it in another way. He could help her find the right guy for her.

He could also try and persuade her that that guy was right in front of her nose.

CHAPTER THREE

SHE spent most of her fourth date with Bryan studying him and comparing him. *To Sean.* Damn the notion that had occurred to her that he looked like him. Because the thought had got stuck in her head and she'd felt the need to make sure that he didn't. Only to end up realising just how short Bryan fell of the ideal that, apparently, was Sean O'Reilly.

It wasn't Bryan's fault. He was a nice guy. A nice, sweet, gentlemanly kind of a guy. But, having now compared him with Sean, Maggie knew that they'd be lucky to make it to a fifth date.

Damn Sean. Not that he'd done anything beyond just being there. In the background, all the damn time of late, as it happened.

Somehow she managed to smile her way through dinner and remain attentive through drinks. But the end of the evening couldn't have come soon enough. She was just going to have to keep looking. Because somewhere out there, there had to be someone who could measure up to what she couldn't have. Ever. No question about it.

Bryan insisted on walking her to the large front door, even though she insisted she knew the way. But she wasn't cruel enough to jump out of his car and run. After all, it was hardly *his* fault.

It was dark, clouds covering what there was of the moon. And, with the large old country house that was divided into apartments being so far from the road, there wasn't even a glow from streetlights. But Maggie knew the way, and even had to reach a hand out to steady Bryan when he stumbled on the edge of the path.

'Sorry.' He smiled at her in the dim light. 'I'm supposed to be making sure that *you're* all right.'

She smiled back, linking her arm through his as they made it to the door. 'We talked about having low lights put along the path but no one has quite got round to it yet.'

'I could help put those in for you.'

'No.' She almost sighed with relief as they reached the bottom step, the low glow of the hall light shining down on them. 'It's fine. Those of us who own apartments here do that kind of thing between us.'

'Well, you've only to ask.'

'I know.' She removed her arm from his and turned to smile up at him. He really was just such a nice guy. Uncomplicated, open, sincere…

'It's fine, really.'

Bryan continued to smile at her. 'I just hope I can make it back to the car in one piece.'

'I could walk you back a little.'

'Now, that would kind of defeat the purpose of my getting out of the car in the first place, wouldn't it?'

'I guess it would.'

There was an awkward silence as Maggie suddenly realised that Bryan was looking at her intently. Oh, God. He was going to try to kiss her, wasn't he?

'Bryan—'

'I just want to say how much I've enjoyed spending time with you, Maggie.' He stepped closer.

Maggie froze. He *was* going to kiss her. Her mind searched frantically for the words to get her out of the inevitable. She could hardly run screaming into the house, having encouraged him for this long, now, could she? He didn't deserve it.

She swallowed hard. One kiss wouldn't kill her. In a way she guessed she owed him. And then she'd find a way to let him down gently. First thing tomorrow.

With a breath she found words. 'You're a very nice person, Bryan.'

'And so are you.' He stopped an inch or two away from her and asked, 'I was wondering if you would mind if I kissed you?'

She smiled weakly. 'That would be all right, I think.'

Lifting his hands, he cupped her elbows and moved his head closer to hers.

Maggie held her breath and hoped fervently he wouldn't try for anything more than a kiss. Her guilt only actually stretched so far.

But all he did was brush his mouth across hers. Then he blinked down at her, his nose close to hers, and said, 'Thank you.'

Maggie blinked back. *That was it?* 'You're welcome.'

Bryan stepped back and released her elbows. 'I had a lovely time, Maggie. I'll call you tomorrow.'

Still blinking in astonishment, Maggie nodded as he turned away. 'OK.'

There was a small scuffle of gravel followed by a brief grunt. Maggie raised her eyebrows. 'You OK?'

'I'm fine!' he called back to her. 'Don't worry. I'm almost at the car now.'

After another few seconds she heard a door open and saw the dim light from the car's interior. Then the engine started and she waved as the headlights spun over her.

She glanced up at the dark sky and sighed.

'Well, he's a keeper.'

Her head jerked in the direction of Sean's voice as he stepped out of the dark and into the circle of light at the door. 'How long have you been there?'

He smiled slowly. 'Since just before that passionate kiss goodnight.'

Her chin rose an inch. 'I had no idea you were into voyeurism.'

'I could take it up with all this romance in the air.' He stepped around her and looked upwards. 'I don't think I've come across a guy so swept up in passion that he took the time to ask *permission* for a kiss and then said thank you afterwards.'

'And I suppose you wouldn't wait to ask?' The words dripped with sarcasm but she wavered when he fixed her with his dark eyes, his smile slow and sensual.

'Hell, no.'

Her mouth went dry.

Sean's smile grew when she didn't come back at him with one of her usual quick answers. 'There's a lot to be said for spontaneity.'

'There's also a lot to be said for good manners.'

He stepped around her again when she tried to move. 'So does he ask permission for everything he does?'

'I'm not answering that.'

'I can just picture it.' He stopped in front of her as he continued in a low drawl, 'I'll just bet he's mannerly every step of the way.'

Maggie clenched her teeth. She wouldn't let him get the better of her. 'He's a very *nice* person. Unlike some people I could mention right now.'

'I'm sure.'

'He's considerate.'

'I'd imagine so.'

She frowned up at him, her eyes sparking. 'He would never do anything I didn't want him to.'

Sean tilted his head to one side and studied her for a split-second. 'Or surprise you with anything that you might enjoy either.'

Maggie's breath caught and without her thinking about it her eyes swept to his mouth.

Sean stepped closer. 'Where's the thrill, Maggie, the passion? How can he get your pulse racing if he asks permission for everything?'

She knew she should have a smart answer for his questions but right at that moment, for the life of her, she couldn't find one. All she could do was watch his mouth as he spoke and feel the air crackle around her.

'Would you mind if I kissed you, Maggie?'

Her eyes shot up to meet his.

'Would you mind if I undressed you a little, Maggie?'

She swallowed hard.

'Would you mind if I took you to bed, Maggie?' He blinked down at her, his dark eyes getting darker. 'Or maybe you wouldn't mind if we just made love right here, Maggie?'

'Stop it.' The words tumbled out on a shaky breath.

'Is that really what you want?' He stepped back from her. 'That cool politeness every step of the way?'

'You have no idea what I want.'

He glanced down, shoving his hands into the pockets of his jeans before he looked back at her. 'Maybe not. But I know what you deserve. And that guy isn't it.'

Maggie felt her lower lip tremble. She would *not* break down in front of him, she couldn't! She couldn't show him that his words had got to her, on many levels. Because every question he had asked had her running hotter than Hades. Because the questions had come from *his* lips and her imagination had provided the mental images to go with them. Bryan had been nowhere in sight, mentally or physically.

With a deep, steadying breath she looked him straight in the eye. 'You have no right to tell me what

I do and do not want from any guy. I make my own decisions.'

'Oh, I know, even when they're bad ones.'

'Because everything you do is just so right all the time, isn't it?' She scowled at him. 'You're just perfect, right?'

'No,' he smiled a slightly lopsided smile at the comment, 'that I'm most definitely not and we both know that I'm not.'

Maggie shook her head. 'No, you're not. But when you reckon you are and all your relationships *are* perfect then you can come and criticise mine.'

'You can't tell me you're seriously considering staying with that guy?' His eyes widened in question.

'That wouldn't be any of your business, would it?' She fumbled inside her bag for her key, her eyes having to look down until she located it. Then she glanced up again, finally rediscovering her spine along the way. 'I'll follow my heart, Sean. Maybe you should try doing the same. That way we both stand a chance of finding the right person for ourselves.'

Sean stepped aside as she walked up the steps, fitted her key in the door and disappeared inside.

He stood for a long time staring at the door. Then he turned and looked out into the darkness.

When he'd come outside for a walk around the house it was because he hadn't been able to sleep, not because he was spying on Maggie. He had needed to think about how he could try and mend their friendship, how he could discover what was bothering her and help fix it. Because he missed her. He really did.

Walking in on her with her 'boyfriend' had been completely unintentional. As had the clenching of his fists when the other man had leaned in to kiss her. If it had gone anything beyond that tepid touch of mouths he might even have unintentionally interrupted them. Or unintentionally felt the need to use one of those clenched fists.

Instead he'd ended up having one of the most sensual conversations of his life.

That conversation, too, might have been at least partially unintentional. But once he'd started he couldn't seem to stop himself. It certainly wouldn't have done anything to help rebuild their friendship. But what it *had* done was open him up to an earlier, small idea of his. One that now grew and took on wings.

The idea of following his heart as Maggie had said and taking a chance, in a roundabout way.

After all, she may not be in love with him now. But that didn't mean he couldn't get her to fall for him, let her see that he could be exactly what she was looking for. That guy who had been right in front of her face all along. He could do that anonymously, without any risk to his pride, because she'd handed him the method. He could try and find out what it was that was bothering her, because she might talk to a stranger in the same way she'd encouraged him to talk in the beginning.

While doing that, he could vet all her other 'candidates'.

Any interference with those candidates along the way would of course, naturally, be *unintentional*.

CHAPTER FOUR

HE WAS 'at' something.

At the morning meeting of crews in the station Sean smiled brightly at everyone, joked around with the other cameramen and flirted with their editor's assistant before plonking himself down next to her with a grin and a 'Hiya' before the briefing started. That action alone made her nervous, for varying reasons.

She felt her body warm when his knee accidentally brushed against her thigh, was aware of every breath he took. She noticed how any movement in the room, displacing the air around them, would bring the scent of his aftershave to her sensitive nostrils.

So she retaliated with coldness. 'Sarah's a bit young for you, don't you think?'

Sean smiled at her stern profile. 'She's legal. What more do I need to worry about?'

'Oh, I don't know…the nuclear fallout that might naturally accompany the break-up of some little affair?' She turned her head to glare at him up close and personal. 'And in the workplace that probably wouldn't be the best career decision you've ever made, now, would it?'

Sean grinned a wolf-like grin at her. 'That

wouldn't be a teeny bit of jealousy there, now, would it?'

Maggie snorted gracefully. 'Dream on.'

He nudged her so suddenly she ended up nudging the guy beside her and had to take a second to apologise. Then she scowled back at him. 'She's twenty-three, Sean; leave her be. Let her discover most guys are snakes on her own.'

Sean focused his eyes forward, his voice dropping as the meeting started. 'Maybe she should date someone with slightly better manners. Someone nice and polite.' He tilted his head to whisper, 'Someone who says *please* before they do anything.'

It took a moment for her to decipher his meaning. When she got it she gaped at him like a goldfish and struggled to find words that her mother wouldn't slap her for saying. The inner struggle distracted her from mundane little things, like the meeting they were in. To the extent that it took two attempts at her name before her eyes focused on their editor.

'You with us, Maggie?'

She flushed. 'Yes, Joe; sorry.'

Joe quirked an eyebrow and handed her a sheet of paper. 'There have been cuts in the fishing quotas so I want you to head to one of those wee ports on the Co. Down coast and see what the locals have to say.'

She nodded as she speed-read what he'd given her:

Usual background stuff, interviews with the families and local shop owners and then something with one of the crews out on a trawler.

Her eyes widened as she glanced up. '*On* the boat? As in *at sea* on the boat?'

'Yes; is that a problem?'

'No.' She shook her head and pinned a smile on her face. 'Not a problem. How long a piece?'

His eyes widened at the question. 'Well, how about you just bring us as much as you can and we'll edit it together? You know, it really depends what else comes up in the headlines.'

He moved on to the next crew and Maggie looked back at the sheet of contacts in front of her. This day just got better by the second. She *hated* boats. Really, truly couldn't stand them. Ever since she'd gone swimming off one as a child. With a little help from her brother's hands in the centre of her back, that was. The fear of water had never left her.

She swallowed hard and glanced at Sean as he leaned in to read over her shoulder. That at least distracted her from the thought of spending some of her day on a *boat*.

'You OK?' He looked at her eyes, close to his, one dark brow rising in question.

'Oh, yeah, just fine and dandy.' She smiled through clenched white teeth.

'Great stuff.' He leaned back, and within a few minutes the meeting broke up and they set off to drive to the east coast.

She had thought the journey would be hell. That after the conversation the night before and his wise-arse comments during the meeting she wouldn't be able to face him. Or stay trapped with him in a car without ending up arguing with him. But it was like none of the previous things had ever happened. In fact Sean was more like they had both been in the good old days, when they got along a whole pile better.

He told her tales about Don and Rachel gardening the day before, with all their little glances and blushes. He talked about how they really should put low lighting along the path to the house, for safety reasons. He whittered away about her sister Kath's new husband and what a great guy he was. But never once did he mention Bryan, their conversation after Bryan had left or how much he disagreed with her method of finding a husband. It freaked her out.

Something was going on.

The initial interviews with families of the trawler crews went smoothly, as did the ones with local businessmen who would see their own livelihoods affected if the fishing crews had to quit. Like every other small community built around the fishing industry, this one knew a cut in quotas could in time lead to the end of the village. And the fear came through as each of the people opened up to Maggie's friendly manner and easy-going questioning.

Then came the thing that Maggie had been dreading for the entire day. It was time to take a trip on the big, wide ocean.

Her stomach churned and she watched the trees on the water's edge shift as the wind picked up.

'It's getting windy.'

Sean glanced up from his camera and followed her gaze. 'Some. Nothing compared to what these guys go out in half the time, though, I'll bet.'

Her stomach churned again. And she hadn't even left the safety of the stone jetty yet.

'They're very brave.'

Sean shrugged. 'It's what they do. I guess they don't see it as anything but doing another day's work.'

A burly man in a bright yellow waterproof coat smiled up at them as they walked to the end of the jetty.

'You must be the TV people.'

Sean grinned and reached a large hand out to shake the other man's. 'Yep, that's us. You must be Mike.'

'Mike McCabe. This here's *The Sally* at the end.'

'I'm Sean O'Reilly, this is Maggie Sullivan.' Sean's eyes drifted to Maggie's pale face, surprised when she didn't greet Mike with her trademark hundred-watt smile. 'She's normally brighter than this.'

Maggie glanced at him and then recovered, smiling as she shook Mike's hand. 'Hi, Mike.'

Mike's ruddy face went even ruddier as she smiled at him. 'Nice to meet you, Miss Sullivan. We see you on the box all the time.'

Maggie's smile faded as he released her hand and turned towards the brightly coloured trawler. The scent of fish hit her nostrils, not exactly helping her churning stomach. 'So this is your boat, then, Mike.'

'Aye.' He beamed with pride as he jumped down

onto the deck and held out his hand to help her aboard. 'This is *The Sally*. My dad's boat and mine now. It'll be my boys' one day if the quotas don't kill us first.'

She gave herself a minute to accustom herself to the movement of the deck beneath her feet. Then the boat rocked as Sean landed beside her with a huge thud of equally huge feet on wood. He glanced at her, his hand cupping her elbow. 'You OK?'

'Oh, I'm great.' She moved into the centre of the boat as the engines started and Mike's crew cast off from the jetty. 'Let's just get this done.'

They went out a lot further than she'd thought they would. And if it had been a tad windy by the water's edge, in the shelter of the harbour, out in the main channel was to her the equivalent of a hurricane.

They started the interview once *The Sally* had thrown out her nets and Sean had got plenty of footage of the crew at work. Maggie managed to get through it. Just. But by the end she had to run to the railing to throw up.

Sean appeared by her side with a bottle of water and rubbed her back. 'You should have said you weren't feeling well.'

She turned from the railing and glanced at him from the corner of her eye. 'I'm not sick.'

'No, course not; you were just considerately feeding the starving fish of the world your breakfast.' He grinned.

A similar grin appeared at the lip of the water bottle. 'You're a funny guy. But I'm not sick, really.'

'I see.' He leaned back against the railing and folded his arms across his chest, his dark hair catching in the wind. 'Well, since you've never mentioned having a problem with boats, then that leaves only one option.'

'Oh, really?' She quirked an eyebrow at him. 'Well, since you're so all damned knowing and seeing, what, pray tell, would that be?'

His eyes sparkled at her as she continued to smile. This was more like normality for them. This easy banter and comfortable proximity. This was the kind of thing he missed.

With a deep breath he winked at her. 'Since I'm the only guy you've slept with these last few months, you must be pregnant. Guess we'll just have to go get married.'

Maggie's smile disappeared, her breath caught in her lungs and her heart twisted agonisingly in her chest. Already emotional about her complete panic being on a boat, *miles* from shore, she found it too much of an effort to hold back the shimmer that appeared in her eyes. She swiftly turned her face from his.

But he'd seen it. 'Hey.' He leapt away from the railing, his arm encircling her shoulders. 'What's up?'

Her eyes glancing out at the choppy waves, she shook her head. 'I'm fine. It's just this boat.'

'You sure?' His voice was soft, persuasive. 'You can tell me, you know.'

She nodded and gripped the railing again. 'I just

really hate boats, that's all.' She glanced at him through watery eyes. 'I can't swim.'

'You can't swim?'

'No.' She smiled. 'Colin pushed me off a boat when I was six and I almost drowned. I'm scared rigid of the water.'

His eyes widened at the new information. 'You should have said.' He hauled her into his arms and tucked her head beneath his chin. 'We could have shot this on the dock.'

'Not unless it was boat-shaped, we couldn't.' She sniffed against his broad chest, forcing herself to open up about one thing when she couldn't about another. 'Joe wanted it done on a boat. And you know I always get the story I'm sent to get.'

'Even when you don't want to get it, huh?'

She risked lifting her head to look up at him. 'Because that's what people like you and me do.'

Something crossed his eyes, then he lifted a hand to tuck her head back into place. 'Sometimes it's just not a big enough deal to cause yourself pain over.'

'And sometimes you just have to get on with it so that it's more real for other people.'

It was ridiculous to mentally compare what they were doing now to what Sean had done for years. But sometimes, when things were difficult for her, Maggie would find herself thinking of what he might have seen and it made her braver, out of a sense of shame if nothing else. How could she be such a chicken about a simple thing like a boat when he'd risked his life dozens of times?

Sean still hadn't really talked much about his years working in battle zones. Travelling from one hell to another. Every time they got close to broaching the subject he would get that look in his eyes, would shut the world out while he remembered. It was that vulnerability that drew her to him time after time. She would feel a tug from her heart, demanding that she offer him comfort of some kind. It pulled her closer to him as their friendship grew, it held her to him. That very vulnerability becoming her vulnerability. What little he talked about only drew her further in.

He took a breath, the rise and fall of his chest beneath her ear a reassuring movement to her troubled soul. It felt so good to be this close to him. Even if it was just for a little moment.

'You still could have told me.'

Her arms lifted and she wrapped them around his waist, her hands smoothing against the back of his heavy jacket. 'It's no big deal. I'll be OK now.'

His arms tightened. 'I'll hold on to you.'

She smiled. 'Promise?'

'Promise.' He rested his cheek against her soft hair, breathing in what he could of her scent through the salty air. He could hold on to her forever if she'd just let him. 'Look, I can even see the dock now.'

Turning her head, she could see the stone edge jutting out into the choppy water, white spray showing as the waves hit it. And for the first time in her life she wished she could stay on the water a second or two longer. Turning away, she snuggled back against his chest. 'Let me know when we're on dry land again.'

He laughed above her head and held her close. 'I will.'

As they entered the calmer water of the harbour it occurred to Maggie, somewhere in the deepest recesses of her mind, that she wasn't so scared with Sean holding her. Somehow she knew it would take a brave wave to pull her out of his arms.

But the chugging of the trawler's engine eventually brought them to the dock and the crew jumped out to tie her fast. So, reluctantly, Maggie stepped back from the security of Sean's arms.

She raised a hand to brush her windswept hair back from her face and smiled shyly up at him. 'Back to safe ground again.'

Sean studied her face long and hard, trying to read the expression in her eyes before she turned away from him. 'You wait here; I'll get the gear off and come get you.'

'I'll be fine—'

'Stay put.'

His stern expression immediately rooted her feet to the deck. He really could be quite masterful when he put his mind to it.

She allowed herself the luxury of watching him as he climbed off the boat, lugging his camera with him as if it weighed the same as a bag of sugar. He moved with casual ease as he set it down against the wall and turned to her with a warm smile.

She smiled back. It really was going to be tough finding another Sean.

Who was she kidding? She watched as his long legs brought him back to her, as he held a large hand towards her. No matter what great guy she found out in cyberspace he just wasn't going to be Sean. She was going to have to learn to live with that. Lower her expectations a little.

Her smaller hand reached out for his and she watched as his long fingers closed around hers. She felt the warm security of his grasp as he helped her onto terra firma. And she kept looking at their hands for a few seconds even when her feet were back on the ground. Because it just felt so right to have her hand there, as though it belonged somehow.

And Sean showed no signs of hurrying to let go. He squeezed her fingers. 'See, safe now.'

'Yes.' She lifted her lashes and looked up into his dark eyes. 'I'm all better now. You always look out for little old me, don't you?'

He nodded slowly. 'I try to.'

She loosened her fingers from his and smoothed her hand along her trouser leg. 'You're a pretty terrific friend.'

Sean stared into her eyes. And there it was again. The sadness, that small, flickering glimpse of the part of her soul that seemed to be dying.

He stepped closer to her, his voice soft and persuasive. 'What's wrong, Mary Margaret?'

Maggie's mouth curved upwards at the edges, her eyes sparkling. 'I'm fine.'

'You sure?'

She nodded. 'I'm sure.'

One of his long fingers reached out and tucked a windswept lock of hair behind her ear. 'You could tell me, you know.'

Maggie took a step back from him and glanced over his shoulder, breaking the hypnotising eye contact. 'I'm fine. Really.' She laughed a small laugh. 'So much better now I'm *off* the boat,' then forced herself to look at him again, 'and I'll be better again when we're in the car with the heater on.'

Sean watched with hooded eyes as she glanced at the car and then back at him. A smile pinned to her lips. Oh, there was something. He knew it as surely as he knew it was necessary to breathe in and out to survive. But he wouldn't push her. Confrontation didn't work. So he would have to let it go. *For now.*

But tonight…tonight was a different matter. He had his window of opportunity now, a chance to get to the bottom of this. He just hoped he'd survive when she found out how he'd done it.

With a smile he leaned down for his camera and took two long strides to catch up with her as she headed for the car. 'We'd better turn the heat on, then.'

Maggie blinked at his smiling face as he opened the passenger door for her with a small flourish. She felt her stomach flutter yet again. Sean O'Reilly was up to something, she could just feel it. She needed to watch out for momentary lapses like these, when her guard would slip and she'd feel safe with him. Because the last thing her heart was around him was safe.

CHAPTER FIVE

'HELLO MaryO, how r u tonight?'

Maggie blinked at the words that sprung up on her screen with an accompanying musical note. It wasn't the first time the 'chat box' had appeared when she'd been browsing the site but usually it had been a message from someone she'd already talked to by e-mail.

This *Romeo34* was someone new, though. She cringed slightly at his on-screen name.

For a moment she considered not answering him, her fingers tapping lightly on the table in front of her laptop. Then they moved to the search button on the top of her screen and she typed in the name to look at his site profile.

Another note sounded. *R U shy?*

She waited for the profile to upload, only to discover it had no photograph. She scrolled down through what he'd written: 'Single dad, 34, two children'. He certainly ticked the right boxes.

If I were u I guess I'd go take a look at my profile be4 I answered. That's ok. I'll wait.'

She scowled at his words. Smart guy.

The lack of a photograph would normally have stopped her in her tracks. It made her nervous. After all, for all the good stories she'd heard about people who met on the internet there were just as many stories of people who lied and spun a fantasy version of themselves.

And Maggie had to be extra-cautious. Because people knew her, saw her face every day on the local news. She was a low-level celebrity in their part of Ireland. The last thing she needed was to become news herself. But part of the reason she'd tried the site had been its success rate with professional people and it wasn't as if she'd been recently nominated for an Oscar or anything. But just to be on the safe side she might have possibly added a *blurred* photograph of herself to her own profile.

'So, do I sound like a stalker?'

She seriously considered not answering him. After all, up until now she had been the instigator of any conversations she'd had through the site. But she was a good Irish girl and her mother had raised her to be mannerly, so it wouldn't be good manners not to speak when spoken to, now, would it?

'How would I know what a stalker sounded like?' Her finger wavered over the return key for a few moments before she bit her lip, closed her eyes and clicked it down.

'Good point. I guess I'd have 2 be around more than five minutes before u knew. I'm reliably informed that stalkers do that.'

He was funny. A smile appeared on her face of its own volition. Funny was good. She typed back that she'd heard that rumour.

'So how's internet dating going 4 u?'

'Ok, thank you.'

'So why here? No nice guys in the real world?'

It was a good question. And one that under normal circumstances she knew she could have denied. There were plenty of great guys in the real world. But the ones that might have made her happy would more than likely have wanted something she couldn't give them. And hence her departure from the singles scene in the real world to the supposedly more controlled environment of internet dates, where she could try to choose someone who was more likely to fit her new circumstances.

'I lead a fairly busy life. This is easier.' The lie flowed off her fingertips.

There were several seconds of silence from the little coloured box. And then the words appeared, *'U really think it's easier 2 find ur soul mate through a computer? There's no 1 at all u've met along the way who made u think u could stay with them 4ever?'*

Maggie's traitorous eyes moved towards the front door of her apartment. She caught herself leaning back in her chair, as if by looking hard enough she could see through the wooden obstruction and across the hallway. Then she swore under her breath. She really needed to stop mentally playing the word-association game.

Turning back to the screen, she typed with angry fingers, *'Obviously not or I wouldn't be on here, would I?'*

'Didn't mean 2 touch a nerve...'

How could he tell that from words typed on a

screen? Pushing back her chair, she walked away from the laptop and stalked into the kitchen to make tea. Sweet tea. Sugar was just a necessary evil occasionally. Musical notes sounded from the computer while she waited for the kettle to boil. They sounded again as she poured boiling water over the bag and swooshed it around with the aid of its string. And one more time as she added milk and gave the spent bag a decent burial in the bin.

He was persistent, wasn't he?

Cup in hand, she sat back down and read his words all in one go.

'It's up 2 u what way u meet people and I 4 1 am glad u're here or I wouldn't be talking 2 u, would I?' Followed by, *'So what r u looking 4 here that u can't find there?'* And then a final, *'R u still there or have I scared u away already?'*

Sipping at her tea she curled one leg underneath her on the chair and considered whether or not to keep talking to him. After all, that was the beauty of the anonymity of the internet. She could just disappear or block him from her life if she chose to. There was a certain safety in that. Safety, but also an all too easy way of allowing herself to hide from people. And that wasn't why she'd decided to do this in the first place, was it?

She was there to try and meet someone. To open herself up to the possibilities outside of her everyday circle. To try and meet someone who could stand up to the ideal that was Sean damn O'Reilly…

So her fingers moved to the keyboard again. *'I'm*

still here. And if I knew what I was looking for wouldn't I already have found it?'

The cursor on the screen flickered while she sipped her tea, then, *'Sometimes what we're looking 4 can b right under our noses.'*

Her heart skipped as the words appeared. It couldn't be, could it?

Then there was another musical note. *'Like a new friend 2 b made...'*

Great, now she was so paranoid she could even imagine Sean in words on a computer screen. She reminded herself to snap out of it and get on with her life. With this great plan of hers. And there was an ideal opportunity in front of her, wasn't there?

With a deep breath and even more determination to rid herself of her own personal 'demon', she started typing,

'So Romeo, no Juliet for you?'

'Depends...'

'On what?'

She laughed when his words appeared: *Whether or not ur name is really Mary.'*

'If it's not, should we just take that as a sign?'

'1 step at a time. Y don't u just tell me something about u...?'

She wondered where she should start with that. Maybe she should start with something simple like her height or hair colour or favourite binge food. Or maybe she should just jump right on in with the big one?

Sipping again at her tea, she pondered where to begin.

He was a smart guy, this one; maybe she should flirt a little first. *'You're the mystery guy here. Why don't you start? What do you do?'*

Again there was a pause for a few minutes, then, *'I teach water sports.'*

Maggie shuddered. Not a good start. *'What kind of water sports?'*

'Sailing, kayaking, that kind of thing.'

It really wasn't going too well, not that he could know that.

The musical note sounded when she was mid-type.

'Oh, and I teach kids 2 swim 2.'

Maggie's mouth turned upwards as she deleted the words she'd been typing and replaced them with, *'Then we might just be a match made in heaven...'*

It was nearly two in the morning by the time she rolled under her duvet. Her eyes were dry from staring at a screen for so long, she'd drunk enough tea to flush her kidneys out for life and she had a new friend. One she actually liked. One with kids of his own and a home. One with a sense of humour and a brain. One who hopefully wouldn't look so bad that she'd still want to try looking out through her front door and across the hall...

Things were looking up.

She smiled as she rolled into a comfortable sleeping position and whispered into the darkness, 'Ha, Sean who?'

CHAPTER SIX

'ANOTHER hot date?'

Maggie wasn't the least bit surprised to find Sean in the reception hall when she came back from a late dinner. He looked as if he'd been caught longer in the summer rain than she had. His dark hair was curling in damp locks against the nape of his neck, his jacket several shades darker than its usual navy.

Shaking her umbrella, she glanced at him from beneath lashes spiked with water. 'Are you spying on me?'

'Oh, yeah, right, 'cos I have nothing better to do with my time.' He started to walk past her to the wide staircase that led to their part of the house.

Maggie followed him. 'Well, you have to admit that every time I come back from a date you're hovering about somewhere.'

Shrugging his wet shoulders, he kept on walking. 'That has more to do with insomnia than it has to do with any interest in your dates.' *Which wasn't entirely true.*

'Since when did you have insomnia?' Giving him a look of disbelief to his back was probably pointless so she sighed and glanced away from his shoulders. This unfortunately brought her observant gaze to his rear as he walked ahead of her. And for the life of her she couldn't seem to look away.

His deep voice echoed off the cavernous ceilings. 'I haven't slept for more than five or six hours in years.'

'Really?' She continued watching his rear as he walked up the last step and onto the corridor. 'How come?'

Sean laughed. 'Is this friendly curiosity or are you going to charge by the hour for your analysis?'

Choosing to ignore his question, she instead focused on how well he filled out a pair of jeans. She'd always thought she was an 'eyes' girl, but wow, she could change her mind. Maybe it was just because, wet as his jeans were, they just moulded in *all* the right places.

At the doors to their apartments he swung round to look at her and grinned when her eyes shot upwards and she blushed. He studied her face for the briefest of seconds and then asked, 'Were you just checking me out?'

'No!' She blushed an even fiercer red at the lie.

'Yes, you were.' He continued grinning as he leaned a shoulder against the wall and folded his arms across his chest. 'So, what's the verdict?'

With a scowl she went searching for her door key, her eyes avoiding his. 'I have better things to do than look at your rear.'

'You *were* looking though.'

'I was not!' As if she was about to admit she had been. Locating the key, she produced it from her bag with a flourish and scowled up at him. 'And even if I *was* I wouldn't be looking at much.'

'Well, that would be a matter of opinion, I guess. You wouldn't be the first person to compliment me on it.'

Why, the smug—! She tilted her chin and quirked an eyebrow. 'I don't think your ego's opinion counts.'

He laughed. And the deep sound echoed along the hallway again. Unfolding his arms, he stepped forwards and took the key from her cold fingers, his face moving dangerously close to hers. 'So, you going to invite me and my superior rear in for hot chocolate to help me sleep?'

Maggie felt his warm breath tickle her skin and her nostrils were invaded with the faint, lingering scent of his way too familiar aftershave. She felt the tiniest bit dizzy for a second. 'Maybe you and your superior rear should just try counting some sheep.'

She reached for her key, only to find her hand enclosed with it in his grasp. She swallowed hard.

'Don't you want to tell me about your date? Friends do that kind of thing, you know.'

Scowling again, she tried to tug her hand free. 'You're not interested in my date, remember?'

'True,' he held his fingers tightly closed around hers, 'but if it's anything like your date with Bryan I might be bored enough to get sleepy.'

Her eyes narrowed. She searched her mind for a suitable retort but, while searching his eyes at the same time, she saw a small flicker. Something she'd seen before. She stopped struggling to free her hand and asked him in a soft voice, 'Why don't you sleep?'

Looking down at their joined hands, he smiled. 'What can I say—when you have as large a brain as mine it's tough to switch it off?'

'You have nightmares?' The memory of him looking haggard on several mornings when he'd overslept invaded her memory.

He shrugged his broad shoulders, moving his fingers absentmindedly over hers. 'It's been known.'

Maggie instinctively stepped closer and bobbed down a little to look up into his eyes. 'How often?'

He raised his dark lashes an inch to meet her curious emerald gaze with a dark one of his own. 'Some.'

'Some, like every time you close your eyes?'

The long fingers eased their hold, but he continued moving skin against skin, his eyes fixed on hers. 'Not if I get good and tired. I sleep pretty well the third or fourth night when it catches up on me. A little past my alarm sometimes.'

Without thinking Maggie freed her thumb and mirrored the movement of his fingers on the backs of his knuckles. 'And the rest of the time?'

His gaze dropped to their hands as he shrugged again. He thought seriously about making another of his usual wisecracks to worm out of an honest conversation. But how could he expect Maggie to ever confide in him if he couldn't still open up to her? It was a two-way street, so he was reliably informed by all the women who had attempted to get him to open up in the past. But it was quite a hurdle to get over. He'd just got so used to dealing with things on his own. Maybe not *coping*, but dealing.

She squeezed her fingers against his. 'Sean?'

His mouth quirked at the edges. 'OK, the rest of the time I might possibly have a bit of an issue with trying not to remember a few things.'

Maggie felt her heart tear a little. Her feet voluntarily made up the last inch of distance between them and she twisted her neck to keep looking into his eyes. She waited until he glanced up at her, his mouth still quirking upwards but his eyes dull. When she spoke again her voice was soft, as soothing as she could make it. 'What do you see?'

He saw Maggie. Right in front of him, close to him. All he would have to do was move his head forward and he could touch his mouth to hers, could lose himself in her and block out the visions that normally tortured him at night. It would be so easy.

If there weren't a part of him that doubted she'd welcome him doing that. And a part of himself that would feel he was using her body to escape the shadows.

He shook his head.

Maggie's eyebrows rose slightly. 'I'm a big girl, you know. I can deal with it.'

'I'm a hell of a lot bigger than you and it's plainly obvious *I* can't deal with it.'

'Then you should talk to a friend about it.'

The quirk of his mouth transformed into a more

genuine smile. 'And you know where I might find one of those, do you?'

She grimaced. 'OK. That was a low blow. But just because we've been a little edgy with each other recently doesn't mean I don't still care.'

'Thanks for caring, Mary Margaret.'

She squeezed his fingers again. 'Then let me make you hot chocolate and we can talk.'

He squeezed back. 'Only if you make a deal with me.'

'What kind of a deal?'

'A swap.'

'Of what?' Her eyes narrowed.

'We're friends, right?'

'Yes, we are.' She still sincerely hoped they always would be. But she could already feel a small gurgle of fear in her stomach.

'And friends can talk to each other,' he paused, 'about anything, I'm reliably informed by a friend I made a while back.'

There had been a time when she'd believed they would be able to do exactly that. But then things had changed. And there were now certain things she couldn't talk to him about. Because if she did he might find out her big secret. And if he found out her secret he might not let her go. She couldn't take a chance on that happening.

Swallowing, she glanced down at their joined hands and then back up into his eyes. She forced herself to remain calm. 'Anything like what?'

He blinked once, twice, his mind working. Then

he smiled. 'If you want me to talk about some of the things that stop me sleeping then you'll be the first person I talk to about it.'

Her voice was husky. 'I'd guess as much.'

It seemed to take an age while he looked deep into her eyes. He searched, asked questions but didn't get any answers. So he went in search of something safer instead. 'So, if you tell me about your dates then I'll tell you what I can about not sleeping.'

She almost sighed in relief. Then she frowned. 'Why would you want to know about my dates? You needn't think you're going to make fun of every single one the same way as you did with Bryan.'

'Wow.' He spoke the word slowly, his mouth becoming a perfect circle for a second. 'Are they all as bad as Bryan?'

'You see, that's exactly what I mean—you just can't help yourself.' She made a feeble effort to free her fingers.

Sean simply tightened his hold, his dark eyes sparkling. 'I promise I'll behave. Can't I be concerned any more?'

'Yes, you can be concerned if you like.' She smiled softly. 'You can be worried, you can tease me, you can do any of those things but it won't change my mind.'

'What have you got to worry about, then?'

Maggie blinked up at him as he unwrapped her fingers, ending up with her door key in his hand. He held it up and snapped his fingers around it while his dark eyes continued to sparkle at her. She should have kicked him in the shins. Because she'd pretty

much agreed to him making any comments he
wanted about anyone she dated. And the last thing
she needed was Sean ripping holes in their person-
alities when she was already so good at doing that
herself.

He tilted his head to one side, then stepped past
her and fitted her key to its lock.

Maggie wanted to know what kept him walking
the halls at night. Because that knowledge was the
kind of thing that had evaded her since they'd met.
She would get a tiny snippet, hints at the awful
truths, snapshots that only made up part of the whole
picture. But he would never completely open up.
And she wanted that, perversely as it would seem.
Because it was yet something more to hold inside
her heart, another piece of the puzzle that was Sean
O'Reilly. Something else to bind her to him in trust
and friendship and therefore something else to make
it difficult for her to walk away from him. She
shouldn't have wanted it, but she did.

He swung open her door and jerked his head to
the interior of her apartment. It was her call. She
could walk inside and close the door on him, shutting
him out for her own safety. Or she could invite him
in, the way she had so many times before.

A dark eyebrow quirked in question.

Hell, she was already lost. She'd been lost for
months. At least if he could open up to her and
maybe unburden some of the things that haunted him
she could leave him with some kind of a parting gift.
She owed him that much. So she walked through the
door, and waited a split-second for him to follow.

CHAPTER SEVEN

'I'LL make some hot chocolate, then.' Peeling off her coat, she walked down the hall as the door clicked behind him.

'I could manage something stronger.'

Switching on the overhead lights in her living room, she turned and looked at him. Her eyes took in the damp hair and the wet jacket he was removing. 'Maybe you should find a towel.'

He glanced across at her. 'Afraid I might leave a mark on your sofa?'

'No, more like that you might catch a cold and be miserable to work with.'

'I'm an excellent patient.'

Maggie laughed. 'Sure you are. But I'm not, so even if you don't mind being wet round the edges, *I'm* going to get changed. Least that way one of us stays healthy.'

She managed to drag her eyes from his and went off to change. Reappearing a few minutes later in comfy jeans and a loose sweater, she found he had switched off the main lights and the room was bathed with the soft glow of table lamps. He was bent over her stereo, searching through CDs with a towel draped around his shoulders.

It wasn't so unusual a scene. It wasn't as if it was

the first time they had disappeared into each other's apartments after a long day and settled down with music to talk over their work, or the people they'd met. But that was the kind of thing they'd done before. It wasn't something they'd done recently. And she felt uncomfortable. Vaguely threatened by his presence in the warm, romantic atmosphere.

His eyes moved in her direction; he hesitated for the briefest moment. And then he stood a little taller and waved a CD in the air. 'Background noise.'

'Good idea.' She moved into the kitchen and searched around for something to drink. Something stronger than hot chocolate he had requested. Wine maybe? It would have to do. She wasn't exactly running an off-licence from her apartment. Pulling a bottle of red from the rack, she grabbed two glasses as soft music sounded from the stereo.

Wine, soft lighting, music. It was more like a date than the date she'd just come back from. 'Entertaining' two men in the one night would have got her quite a name for herself thirty or forty years ago.

Assuming he'd take his usual place in the large armchair closest to the stereo, she sat down on one end of the sofa and poured the wine. But as she did, the seat dipped beside her and she looked up with wide eyes to find him disturbingly close.

The basic instincts inside her yelled she should move. As far away from his proximity as possible. But her stubborn streak demanded she stay put. *Don't be intimidated by him.*

He reached a long arm close to her body to claim a glass before looking her in the eye. 'So, you first.'

'Why do I have to go first?'

He shrugged his wide shoulders. 'Because I'm an old-fashioned kind of a guy and I believe in ladies first…'

Quirking an eyebrow at the statement, she lifted her own glass, curled her legs beneath her, *between them*, and pushed herself further into the plump cushions. 'What do you want to know?'

He shrugged. 'We could start with a name.'

'Paul.'

'Paul. That's a good name. Short and to the point. So what's he like?'

Not like you. She'd given up on the theory of finding someone like Sean and gone with the opposite end of the scale idea. Where Sean was dark, Paul was a sun-kissed blond. Where Sean was brooding, Paul was open. It had made perfect sense to her. 'He's a great guy from what I've seen so far.'

'First date?'

'Yes.' She took a sip of wine.

'Mmm. That can be the make-or-break date, can't it?'

She smiled softly. 'Spoken by the king of dating. So I guess you'd know right enough.'

Sean smiled back at her, 'What can I say? You may not have noticed what a great guy I am but some women do.'

'I'd noticed.' She'd certainly noticed the women who had noticed.

His smile remained, his voice low as he answered with, 'Well, that's something.'

He might have interpreted her answer differently. Her green eyes blinked at him for what felt like an eternity, while he blinked back at her. She hid her face in her glass for a second, then raised her eyes and asked, 'So, how long have you been having bad dreams?'

The smile faded and he lowered his eyes to study his own glass, swirling the contents around. 'They started about six months before I came home. Occupational hazard, I'd guess. Stress-related, unresolved issues.' He glanced back up, his mouth twisting. 'I know the reasons, I just can't seem to shake them.'

And if the truth had been spoken aloud, worrying about and fantasising about Maggie wasn't exactly helping any.

'Have you thought about maybe seeing someone about them?' The question was a simple one. It was what people did these days. There was no reason for someone to suffer in silence in the modern era, even if visiting a psychiatrist wasn't as common an occurrence on their side of the Atlantic as it was on the other.

Sean laughed. 'Nah. I really don't think talking about issues from my childhood will solve the problems of the world.'

Maggie's eyes widened. 'You have issues from your childhood?'

She had met most of his family and from what she

had seen there was as strong a bond there as there was in her own ridiculously large clan. They both came from traditional large Irish families. Both were lucky enough to have parents still around and still happily married. Both had their share of nosy siblings and noisy nieces and nephews. It had never entered her head that he might have issues from his childhood.

'Nothing beyond the times when my older sisters tried dating my friends, so, no.'

'So, is it a case of not wanting to talk to someone you don't know or just not wanting to talk full stop?'

His smile quirked a little more on one side than the other, vaguely hinting at a hidden grin. 'You know me better than I like to think you do.'

Better than was sane. She'd known that much for some time.

She saw the flicker in his eyes again before his smile faded altogether and he looked away. She also knew him well enough to know that when he wasn't looking someone directly in the eye it meant he'd either lost interest or he was hiding something.

'It was rough over there.'

He nodded. 'Yes, it was.'

'You saw some things you'll never forget.'

'No matter how hard I try,' he took a breath and looked her in the eye again, 'and I don't think it's right that I forget. Because if I forget altogether it's like cheating all those people somehow. I was there to make sure the rest of the world, the people back here, knew what was going on. By blocking it out I'm denying all that I tried to show them.'

His words made sense. And Maggie understood, even though she'd never been in any of those places herself. What he'd done for all those years mattered, was important above and beyond anything she'd ever done. She had a world of respect for him because of it.

'But it must have been hard for you not to look away. To try and get some peace for a few moments.'

Sean smiled at her understanding. 'That's why I came home. I guess maybe it takes someone stronger than me to stay there and keep going.'

Maggie's eyebrows folded downwards. 'You think you're not strong? It took guts to go to the places you went to. I couldn't have done it.'

'If you'd had those things right in front of you you'd have done exactly what I did. You're a pro, Mary Margaret. We do what we do.'

Her brow softened and she smiled. 'It's hardly the same thing. All I do is local-interest stuff. Everyday things and everyday people.'

'And that matters too.' He reached out a long finger and brushed her hair back from her shoulder, his eyes momentarily distracted from hers. 'Because in understanding the people next to us we help to breed tolerance. And that means a lot these days. It means people can be outraged and upset when they see the kinds of things I saw in Somalia or Ethiopia or Iraq. They need the small things to matter so that the big things are worth fighting for.'

Her heart fluttered as his finger lingered in her hair, her pulse jumped when his eyes looked back into hers. She swallowed, hard, her throat convulsing. 'Does being home help?'

He thought about it for several breaths. 'Yes.'

'But you still have the dreams.'

A small smile, then, 'Yes.'

'Maybe you just need to give it more time, time for happier memories to overshadow the bad ones.'

'Could be.'

She was being pulled in again, she could feel it. As surely as the moon pulled at the tide. His dark eyes stared into hers, holding her fixed in place like a rabbit in the headlights of a car. If he wanted to he could move his head close to hers, fill the space between them and draw her into his arms. And Maggie knew she would find it tough to stop him.

With a shaky breath she uncurled her legs and leaned forward, stretching her glass towards the chest she used as a coffee-table. She needed a little distance. For safety's sake.

But a large hand on her arm halted her escape. 'Where you going?'

Her eyes focused on his hand rather than looking back into his eyes. 'You hungry? I'm hungry. I thought I'd get some crisps or something.'

'I'm not hungry.'

His deep voice seemed awfully close. She risked a sidewards glance and found him *dangerously* close. Her heart fluttered again. This had been a bad idea.

While he repeated her move and placed his glass

on the chest, the thumb against her arm began to move back and forth. His dark eyes stayed focused on her, his voice dropping intimately. 'Didn't Paul feed you?'

She nodded.

'Did he ask permission to kiss you goodnight like Bryan did?'

She shook her head.

With a tug on her arm he pulled her back into the cushions, his eyes searching hers. 'Did you want him to?'

She swallowed. 'How can I know that after one date?'

He smiled slowly. 'You should know it after about sixty seconds. It's called attraction.'

Oh, she knew what attraction was. She was experiencing it up close and personal right that second as it happened.

'Sometimes it takes longer than sixty seconds to know you want someone.' She made an attempt at levity. 'Slow and steady wins the race, as my dad would say.'

His smile grew. 'Is that right?' Encouraged by the fact that she hadn't tried to struggle out of his hold, he let his hand stray down her arm towards her hand. 'He may have a point. There's a lot to be said for taking a little time.'

Her head told her she should be moving away from him. But as usual her heart and her body were reluctant to let go. Thankfully, he didn't do what she so badly wanted him to do. He didn't take the opportunity to move closer. And that was enough time for her to pull her arm free. 'I'm prepared to take it slow with Paul, and with anyone else I might meet this next while. I know the right one will come along.'

Sean's smile faded slightly. 'And yet you're still determined to be married to some stranger within the year.'

She nodded, her eyes moving away from his. 'Yes, if I meet the right one.'

'Why now?'

The question hung in the air like a poison, making every breath she took seem tainted somehow.

'I have my reasons.'

'Reasons that you won't discuss with me.'

She pulled herself up from the sofa and put some distance between them, the emotional distance already widening again. 'Reasons I won't discuss with you.'

'Why not?' He leaned forward, his elbows resting on his knees. 'You've always been so keen to get me to open up and now, when I do, you shut me out in return. Why?'

With a swift turn of her heel she spun to look down on him from the other side of the room, her eyes sparkling in the soft light. 'Because there are some things I can't talk about. Things you wouldn't understand.'

His face remained calm. 'Try me.'

Maggie stood a little taller. 'I think you should go. Try and get some sleep.'

'Maybe I don't want to go. Has it occurred to you that the reason we've been arguing so much recently is that I care about you, that just maybe I would like to try and help?'

Despite the raise in his voice and the hurt in his eyes she knew what he was saying was true. And another little part of her died, having to shut him out.

She kept her voice calm, controlled. 'I know you care. But if you care you'll let this go.'

The world seemed to stop turning while he stared up at her, slowly unwound his large body from the sofa and stood looking at her with those damned dark eyes of his.

Then he shook his head and smiled. 'No can do.'

As he stepped towards her Maggie instinctively stepped back. He stepped forward again, she stepped back. Her eyes widened in panic and she glanced around the room, feeling the sudden need to discover something she could throw at him. Meanwhile he kept on coming.

Her eyes moved back to his face and were immediately drawn to the curve of his mouth. If she ever made the mistake of kissing him she'd be lost.

His eyes continued to watch her retreat. Then after a couple more forward steps that were immediately followed by Maggie's backtracks, he seemed to come to a decision. He took a breath, ran a hand back through his hair and looked her in the eye. 'I won't leave this be because I can't.'

Breathless, she asked with a shaky voice, 'Why not?'

With a steady gaze and a steady tone he answered, 'Because I just care too much to let you make a mistake this big. And it's been a long time since I cared this much.'

CHAPTER EIGHT

'HAVE u ever been in love?'

Maggie thought long and hard about the question. And how to answer it. She'd been talking to Romeo online for nearly a week now and even though Paul was a nice guy she kept on coming back to her night-time talks with this mystery guy.

She liked to think of it as keeping her options open. But what it really told her was that Paul wasn't 'the one' any more than Bryan had been.

'I'd be pretty sad if I'd got to my age and not felt that somewhere along the line.'

'Now, that's not exactly answering my question, is it?'

The irritating musical note that heralded his words never ceased to make her heart miss a beat. She was never quite sure what he would say next. Whether he would crack a joke that would have her smiling long after she'd signed out, or whether he would be asking a question that would delve into her best-kept secrets. Maybe it was that touch of unpredictability that kept her coming back for more. Or maybe it was just the old-fashioned romance that accompanied the mystery of him. Who knew?

'I've had my heart broken a time or two.'

She lifted her bottle of water and curled her feet

beneath her as she waited for his answer, music playing in the background. It was something they did
now; they would set the mood. One or the other of
them would pick a track or two of music, or a particular album they liked and they'd play it in the
background while they 'talked'. It was almost as if
they were in the same room sometimes.

The note sounded. *'Recently?'*

Balancing the laptop on her thighs, she answered
with, *'Yes, fairly recently.'*

'Tell me about him?'

It was a biggie. In her experience, talking to a
'new' someone about an 'old' someone could inevitably lead to disaster. It was the age-old question of
how much to disclose without breeding contempt.

*'There's not much to say beyond the fact that it
wouldn't have worked out.'* She sipped at her water
again before setting it back on the chest.

*'Relationships can b tough these days. Sumtimes
we don't know wat we want till it's right in front of
us.'*

That was so true. She knew it only too well. Her
fingers began to type their answer but were interrupted by yet another note. *'So what was it that convinced u it wouldn't work? U get dumped?'*

She laughed aloud. 'Yeah, like my life is that simple.'

Her fingers worked on removing the words she'd
started before she retyped, *'I had to let him go. I
could never have given him what he needed.'*

He didn't answer straight away so she allowed herself a moment to close her eyes, her head leaning back into the plump cushions as the soft music filled her ears. Whatever else her Romeo may be, he was a romantic when it came to his choice of music. Maggie had never been a fan of classical music, but the violins seemed to tug at a part of her soul she had denied before.

A 'non-classical' note brought her out of her reverie. *'Sorry, nature called. But I'm back. Miss me?'*

She smiled again. He could be such a guy sometimes.

'Now, where were we? Oh, yes, u could never give him what he needed. What was that, then? He in2 something weird?'

'Not that I'm aware of, but then I guess it depends on your definition of "weird". Some weirdness might be OK.'

'I knew I liked u 4 a reason.'

'Don't even go down that road. I'm just beginning to like you some.'

'Then I better b on my best behaviour.'

'Yes, you had.'

Sometimes when she talked to him it felt as if she'd known him forever. It shouldn't have felt natural, should have had that edge of awkwardness that she'd felt when she'd first started talking to any of her other 'candidates', but it just didn't. This guy just…fitted. He gave her hope.

'R u telling me this guy was needy?'

Maggie laughed aloud again. As if he'd ever allow that description of himself to be aired publicly. He wasn't needy, well, not in the sense that her Romeo probably meant. He needed. There was a difference.

'Not needy. There were just things that he wanted and deserved that I couldn't give him. It wasn't his fault.'

She waited again.

'Do I get a clue?'

'You're the smart guy, maybe I should just give you something to think about.'

'Oh, I c, a mystery. Now I'm intrigued. From what I've learnt so far I don't c that there's anything wrong with u, Mary.'

Her fingers hesitated. Soft music tried its best to soothe her soul. Was it time?

'The world is full of flawed people. I just happen to be flawed, that's all. Maybe when I know you better and I can trust you not to run a mile I'll tell you.'

'I'm not going anywhere.'

Maggie pulled a face. *'You may say that now. But soon you'll not chat as much, then the e-mails will gradually start to fade, and then the next thing I know you'll be back on the site with a change of name and requirements in your profile that are quiet digs at me.'*

There was a substantial pause.

Then, *'I guess if u ever want some 1 2 take as big a chance on u as u're prepared to take on them u have 2 make a leap of faith.'*

It was a pretty damned big leap. Inside a week she knew that her new friend had a family, thought as much of family as she did. His kids were his world.

It was one of the many things on a rapidly growing list that had drawn her to him night after night when she really hadn't intended signing on to the site.

But he was right and his words were like an echo of the conversation she'd had recently with Sean. How could she continue to hold back the truth from this guy when he was so open with her? There had to be trust somewhere. It was important. And maybe she could make amends with one 'relationship' when she couldn't with another.

Because if she was ever going to make a real, lasting relationship with one of the people from her nice, safe virtual world then she had to eventually open up herself. That was how it worked. It was exactly that leap of faith. A hope that there was someone out there that would understand, and accept her the way she was. Flawed as she was.

This Romeo deserved that. Before she got any more attached to him than she already was.

OK. But if you disappear then you know at some point I'll e-mail you with an I TOLD YOU SO...'

He should have had a guilty conscience. But if being devious was what it took then so be it. Means to an end and all that...

All it had taken was one phone call to Kath and amidst some general topics of conversation he had soon found out where Maggie had her dinner reservations with Paul. One quick afternoon of flirting with Joe's young assistant was then all it had taken for Sean to have a date of his own. Then the finishing touch had been a phone call. To the very restaurant where Maggie and Paul were headed.

As he walked through the crowded restaurant his eyes searched for a familiar shining auburn head of hair. And when he found it he could have sighed with relief. Because the incessant chatter from his 'date' had driven him crazy within ten minutes of her sitting in his car.

He placed a hand to the small of her back and guided her through the tables until they 'accidentally' ended up at Maggie's side, the *maître d'* in tow.

'Well, well, what have we here?'

Maggie's eyes widened in surprise as she glanced up when his voice sounded. 'What are you doing here?'

'We're having dinner, same as you apparently.' He grinned lop-sidedly before turning his gaze to the man across the table from her. 'You must be Paul.'

Paul politely shook the hand that was offered and smiled back up at Sean and his date. 'Yes, that's right. And you are?'

With her focus training itself on the woman at Sean's side, Maggie missed the raised eyebrow aimed in her direction.

Sean noticed her look and grinned even more. 'I'm Sean O'Reilly; I work with Maggie.' He freed his hand and moved it to his 'date's' back to propel her forward. 'And this is Sarah; she works at the office with us.'

Sarah smiled and offered her hand, her eyes moving to Maggie. 'Hello—what a wonderful surprise seeing you here. Have you been here long?'

Maggie opened her mouth and then closed it as Paul answered with a, 'No, not long; we've just ordered. Maybe you'd like to join us?'

Maggie glared at him as Sean quickly answered, 'We'd hate to disturb you…'

'No, not at all; it would be nice to meet some of the people that Maggie works with.' He quirked an eyebrow in Maggie's direction that made it difficult for her to yell 'NO!' loudly. Damn the man for being so polite. And damn Sean for turning up on the night she had been going to let him down gently.

'Well, since you insist.'

In the blink of an eye the efficient restaurant staff had two extra chairs and place settings sorted out. And Maggie had no escape.

Sean's thigh brushed against hers beneath the table and she almost shot upright at the contact. Oh, this was just great.

Menus magically appeared and Sean continued to avoid her eye contact and focused instead on Paul. 'So what's the food like in here?'

'I've heard it's very good. I've never been here myself. I live down in Co Louth.'

'A handy drive with all the motorways now, though.'

'Yes, it is.'

'I'm from Co Louth.' Sarah's eyes lit up with enthusiasm. 'Where do you live exactly?'

Paul smiled openly. 'Just outside Dundalk.'

'No way!' She leaned closer to him, her chest directly in his line of vision. '*I'm* from Dundalk!'

Sean vaguely listened as they started to ask who knew whom and then his attention strayed to Maggie. She was staring at Paul and Sarah with a stunned expression. Then she shook her head a barely perceptible amount and turned her gaze on him. There was a spark in her eyes, a tiny vertical frown line between her brows, and then she glared at him with enough venom to make a lesser man shrink down in his chair.

But Sean was bigger than that. He simply continued to grin before blinking at her and saying, 'Hi.'

Maggie gaped at him. 'Hi'? That was all he had to say? She'd give him 'hi'!

CHAPTER NINE

Two hours later she found herself standing outside the restaurant, *alone*, with Sean.

She folded her arms across her chest and watched the car pulling away from them. 'You did that on purpose.'

'What?' He blinked innocently. 'Made Paul volunteer to take Sarah home? They both had Mrs. Leary as an English teacher in first year, you know.'

'Oh, I know. And I also know that Paul's younger brother dated Sarah's second cousin for years and that Sarah's best friend in school works at Paul's uncle's bakery. But I still think that, *somehow*, you knew this would happen.'

He blinked again when she turned her head to glare up at him. 'And how exactly would I know that without the aid of a private investigator?' He took a split-second to add, 'Do we even have those over here?'

Maggie turned slightly to look up at him with narrowed eyes. 'So you just happened, *unintentionally*, to pick this place to eat with your date, did you?'

'Maybe, like you and Paul, I'd heard about all the write-ups this place has had and decided to give it a try.'

'You were trying to impress the college student?'

She smiled sarcastically. 'Wouldn't a bowl of pasta and a bottle of wine with a screw top have done it for you? I thought all students lived on pasta?'

Despite the fact her sarcasm regarding Sarah actually encouraged him to think he had some hope, he simply blinked back at her with a cool, noncommittal stare. 'It's not my fault they hit it off.'

And about that much he was at least being sincere. Who could have guessed he'd manage to bring someone whom Paul would relate to so quickly? If it hadn't been for three courses of mouth-watering food Maggie and he would have had nothing to do for two hours but watch them chatter away. Sean himself had never actually met two people who could talk so much and still manage to eat at the same time.

'I still think you turned up here on purpose.' She glared at him through narrowed eyes before unfolding her arms and starting down the pavement with a determined stride. 'And nothing you can say will convince me I'm wrong.'

'Whoa there one minute.' He caught her with one long stride, his hand on her elbow halting her progress. 'If I managed to pick the same restaurant as you then it was entirely unintentional.' *Lie number one.*

She looked at him with disbelieving eyes.

'If the *maître d'* happened to bring us by your table that was hardly my fault.' *Lie number two.*

Her eyebrows quirked as she glanced away.

'And there's no way I could have known they'd both know that many people. I mean, c'mon, Maggie,

I'd never even met Paul before tonight—' that much was true; *lucky*, but true '—and I'm hardly likely to have invited a sexy young thing like that out on a date in order to bump into you, now, am I?' *And three made the hat trick.*

Maggie seemed to study the other passers-by on their pavement for an inordinate amount of time before her eyes eventually strayed back to his. 'And yet here we are.'

He smiled. 'Yes, here we are.'

She continued to look up at him.

'It's fate, that's what it is.'

A ladylike snort of laughter escaped her. Then she pulled her arm free and started to walk again.

Sean followed by her side, his long strides matching hers. They walked past the floodlit City Hall, each of them ignoring the stately opulence of the building they saw every day. Then eventually Sean asked, 'So where are we going now?'

Maggie sighed. 'I haven't the faintest idea.'

They continued walking. Then he spoke again. 'Can I make a suggestion?'

'Only so long as it involves finding your car and going home.' She stopped dead in her tracks. 'You *were* good enough to actually pick up your date for the evening, right?'

Stopping in his tracks, he turned to look back at her. 'No, I made her hitchhike to the restaurant.'

'I actually wouldn't put that past you.'

'Funny.' He stepped closer and blinked down at her, her face illuminated to his eyes by the streetlights. 'Don't Kath and Michael normally go to the comedy night at the Empire on a Tuesday night?'

His question caused her to frown for a moment as she thought. 'Yes, I think so; why?'

He nodded. 'OK, then.'

Before she knew it he had her elbow once more and was steering her along the footpath. 'Hey, maybe I want to go home.'

'Where's your sense of adventure?' He looked down at her with a sexy grin that turned her knees to mush. 'Maybe you'll meet the man of your dreams there.'

'Why, do you have another chesty twenty-something for him to leave with?'

'Nope, this time there's just you and me.'

That was what worried her...

'It's good to see you two are getting along so well.' Kath had to lean in close to yell in Maggie's ear when Sean disappeared to the bar with her husband, Michael.

Much against her better judgement she'd allowed him to drag her along to the Empire, but as it turned out she was having a great time. The comedians were hilarious, the atmosphere was upbeat, and thanks to her sister and brother-in-law they even had seats. Which was a miracle in itself.

'It takes a bit of effort,' she yelled back.

'But it's worth it, isn't it?' was the yelled reply.

It was. When they were in an atmosphere like this or working together like the well-oiled team that they had used to be, things were simple. It was only when she was forced to spend time alone with him that things got difficult.

She laughed aloud at the latest comedian's punch-lines and then she found her eyes straying from their seats in the balcony to the crowded bar, where she could just about see Sean. She watched him laugh with Michael, saw the manly bonding of a slap on the back and she smiled. If her life had only been simpler she could have spent hours just looking at him.

Kath's eyes studied her for a long moment, and then she leaned in again. 'So what's wrong with him?'

Her eyes were still focused on his dark-haired head, the set of his shoulders, the way the muscles in his arm moved as he reached money to the bartender. Then she looked at her sister.

'What?'

Kath smiled. 'Why isn't he husband material?'

Maggie frowned. 'I didn't say he wasn't. He just isn't for me.'

'Why?'

Raucous laughter surrounded them again before she could lean close enough to yell, 'You just won't let this go, will you?'

Her sister's shoulders shrugged.

'I have my reasons,' she yelled again.

'Then tell me!' was the yelled reply.

'I can't, Kath!' She saw the look of hurt in eyes the same shade she saw every morning in the mirror and she softened, her hand reaching out for Kath's arm. 'Not here, anyway. I was scared if I told you it might bring up a lot of bad stuff for you. And I didn't want to do that.'

The hurt turned to concern. 'How bad is it?'

Sean and Michael reappeared with their drinks and Maggie only had time to raise a warning eyebrow at her sister and lean in to yell, 'We'll talk soon, I promise.'

Kath scowled, and then recovered quickly to produce her usual besotted smile for her husband.

Another yelled voice sounded in her ear. 'See, I told you you'd have fun.'

She managed a smile for Sean. 'I guess you had to be right at some point.'

'I'm always right.' He leaned in closer to talk in her ear, his head tilting. 'You just hate it when I am.'

Her laughter just about caught his ear, but he could see her shoulders shake. With a smile he leaned in again, this time close enough to smell her hair, the sensual tones of her perfume. 'You see, now, this is the stuff I miss.'

She nodded when he leaned back, his face still close to hers. 'Me, too.'

His face remained close to hers for another moment before he moved back a little. Then, between bursts of laughter, they joined in a shouted conversation with Kath and Michael until the lights came up at the end of the show.

Outside the old building they exchanged hugs, kisses and manly handshakes. Kath hung on to

Maggie for a long time before whispering in her ear, 'I'll come see you soon and we'll have that talk.'

Maggie smiled nervously as she leaned back. 'Sure.'

'I'll call you.'

Sean and Maggie then stood and watched as they walked away. Sean turned his head and looked down at her. 'What was that about?'

Maggie shrugged. 'Sister stuff.'

'OK. Can I interest you in a lift home, then, Mary Margaret?'

Her mouth turned upwards while she looked at him from beneath her lashes, a twinkle of mischief in her eyes. 'Now, there's the kind of invitation I was looking for several hours ago.'

'Forget it, lady; you had a good time and I know it.' He crooked his arm towards her with a minute bow of his head. 'Shall we walk?'

With the softening of senses brought on by several glasses of wine she linked her arm through his and they began the walk to his car. They moved in a compatible silence for several blissful minutes before he spoiled it for her by asking, 'So, any more dates coming up?'

She sighed. 'Why, you need to know where I'll be so you can gatecrash again? Maybe I should just do a schedule out for you.'

He squeezed her arm with his. 'Now, don't go ruining this special moment of peace and quiet with spite. I'm just trying to make some conversation.'

'Mmm.' She didn't believe that for a second.

'I've decided to help you out, as it happens.'

'Oh, really.'

'Yep; it's not like you've had much luck choosing them on your own.'

Somehow the idea of Sean helping her out with her dating choices didn't sit well on her shoulders. 'I'll manage.'

'C'mon, Mary Margaret, where's your sense of adventure? Women never ''get'' men the way another man would. It's that whole Venus and Mars thing.' He smiled ahead of himself. 'I can help you sort the wheat from the chaff.'

'I'm not trying to find someone for you to drink beer with on a Saturday night, I'm looking for someone for *me*.'

His head turned towards her. 'You still need whoever he is to get on with your friends and family and who better to judge that than someone your friends and family already love?' He nudged her with their joined arms. 'C'mon, give it a go. Name me one that you haven't actually met yet who sounds like a potential.'

One name jumped into her head straight away. And for a moment she really felt like starting an argument and dropping the subject. But it was the first time they'd managed to go a few hours without a disagreement of some kind or her being completely focused on his proximity, so she was loathe to kill the moment. Maybe it would even help to salvage some of their friendship, as he'd reasoned.

'There is one, I guess.'

'Great, let's try him on for size. What does he do?'

She frowned at his enthusiasm. 'He works with kids mostly, but he doesn't talk about his work that much.'

'That can be a good thing; means he can focus on the more important stuff.'

'Like what exactly?'

Another nudge. 'Like you, you genius. Next…'

'He's divorced, two kids that live with him—'

'Where's the ex?'

'I don't know.'

He tutted. 'You need to check that out. He might have murdered her and she's under the floorboards. Or, worse still, he doesn't talk about her 'cos he's not over her. Does she visit much…will she be stopping by every day for dinner?'

Maggie stopped walking and turned an inch or two to look up into his eyes. 'You know what my cooking is like. If she stopped by for dinner every day she'd be lucky to live past twenty-four hours. And I'm fairly sure she's not under the floorboards.'

'You can tell whether or not he's a serial killer from his picture?' Sean's eyes widened in question.

Maggie immediately felt her cheeks warm. She averted her eyes and started walking again, her lips pursed.

Sean stopped her and leaned his face towards hers. 'You have seen his picture, right?'

She pursed her lips tighter.

He laughed aloud. 'You're kidding! You're chatting away to this guy and you don't even know what he looks like? He could have two heads or be ninety or some spotty teenager having a few kicks on the net.'

'He doesn't come across like that. He's smart, funny, insightful.'

'A smart, funny, insightful, one-eyed old pirate whose picture has a set of numbers along the bottom?'

She tried to tug her arm free, scowling when he held on to her. 'You see, this is exactly why I don't talk to you about this kind of thing.'

'Maggie, you can't start a relationship with some guy online when you know virtually nothing about him. For your own safety if nothing else you should at least know the basics.'

'I know as much as I need to know for now.'

He leaned his head down again, his dark eyes softening as he stared into hers. 'Promise me you won't try to meet this guy before you know more. Ask him a few more leading questions first; ask to see a photo.'

His words made sense. And she wanted badly for them not to. Because she didn't want to discover that her Romeo was a fake. She liked him, looked forward to their talks and when she thought about meeting him she actually got a tremor. And anyone whose name wasn't Sean O'Reilly who could do that to her was someone she definitely wanted to meet.

But she did have to think about the stalker mentality too. The fact that Sean cared enough to be concerned for her made her take a moment to think about it.

'Maggie, promise me.'

She nodded, smiled, patted the arm that held on to hers. 'I will. I promise. Thank you for caring.'

'Always.'

He looked at her with such intensity that for a moment her knees turned to mush again. Then he simply smiled, turned away and started them along the last steps to his car.

He smiled as he opened her door. Yep, it had been a pretty great night all told. His work was done for another evening. Undermining Maggie's dates was proving much more enjoyable than he could have foreseen.

Now he just had to figure out a way to get her to trust the simple fact that he was the right guy for her. No matter what she might have told herself, and why.

In the meantime he'd make do with undermining the 'opposition'. One step at a time and all that. Maggie wasn't all that immune to him, and somehow the fact that she still wanted him around was all the encouragement he needed.

CHAPTER TEN

SOME days she hated her job.

Today was one of those days. She'd spent the entire time wandering through the Mourne Mountains with a bunch of sixth-form pupils doing an outward-bound course and it had rained the whole damn time. So now she was soaked through, her legs were killing her from all the walking, her hair was sticking out in every direction conceivable and she had blisters on both heels.

With hindsight, breaking in her hiking boots beforehand might have been a good plan. But hindsight was always a useful thing *after* the fact.

Sean meanwhile had had the time of his damned life. Eight hours in the presence of seventeen-year-old girls had done his ego the world of good. And he had walking boots that looked as if they'd probably trekked to Everest base camp without even a hint of a blister. Maggie had hated his guts by lunch time.

Then to top her day off Kath was waiting for her at her door.

'Dear lord, what happened? Where you in an accident?' Her eyes widened in concern as Maggie limped towards her.

Maggie grimaced. 'It feels like I was run over by

a bus. But no, I just went for a wee bit of a walk is all.'

'Where to? Dublin? You look like hell.' She moved away from the door to allow Maggie to open it. 'Let's get you under a shower and in nice comfy pyjamas and we'll have our girl talk.'

Maggie dutifully opened the door and peeled her feet out of their instruments of torture before looking Kath in the eye. 'Do we have to do this now?'

'Yes, we do.' She shoved her along the hallway. 'You're not getting out of this. You've had something major going on in that head of yours for months now and it's about time you spilled it.'

It was just too much after the day she'd had. Her eyes filled with tears as she turned to face her sister in the living room. 'I don't know if I can do this tonight.'

Kath stared in shock as her oh-so-controlled sister dissolved in front of her eyes. She leapt forwards and hauled her into a hug. 'Sweetie, what is it? It can't be that bad.'

'Yes, it is.' She sobbed against her shoulder, the comfort zone of her brain vaguely recognising the same scent of fabric softener that their mother had used when they were growing up. 'I just didn't know how to talk to you about it. And I wanted to, Kath, I really did.'

Kath rubbed her back and held her tight, her voice soothing. 'Then you should have come to me sooner. I can take anything you throw at me; I just can't cope when you go all secretive.' Leaning back a few inches, she dropped her head to look up into Maggie's tear-filled eyes. 'We've always talked, you and me. You know that.'

Maggie managed a nod, but she couldn't find words.

'You're tired, and hungry too, I'll bet.' Her arms squeezed around Maggie's body again. 'Go get a hot shower and get comfy and I'll make us some pasta or something. You'll feel better then, you'll see.'

She doubted it. And if she'd used food as comfort every time she'd felt this bad in the last few months she'd weigh about five hundred pounds by now. But she freed herself from the safety of her sister's arms and limped down the hallway. Tonight had been a long time coming.

A warm shower, requisite comfy pyjamas and a bowl of pasta did strengthen her somewhat. They chatted about how their work days had gone, about what their other siblings were up to, almost as if they were working their way up to the big one. And Maggie was grateful for that.

But it was time. She'd never been as adept as Sean at keeping secrets and maybe if she shared this secret then Kath would get off her case and she'd have one less person to be guarded around. Surely that would help?

'Are you happy now?'

The soft question caught her sister off guard and Kath took a moment to stare and blink before setting her fork down and asking, 'Why is that important in whatever's wrong with *you*?'

Maggie shrugged. 'I guess I just need to know. You had it rough for a long time.'

Kath nodded, her eyes dropping to her almost empty plate. 'Yes, I did, but that's done. Everything happens the way it's meant to. I wouldn't trade Michael for anything.'

Maggie pushed her plate away and wandered across to her favourite soft armchair, the one that Sean usually stole when he was there. 'I used to look at you when you were with Tony and just wish I could make everything better for you. That I could fix it.'

Kath grimaced. 'There was just no making it right in the end. There were too many cracks in our relationship to survive the emotional trauma of the treatments. Michael is different, though.' She smiled as she moved across the room and sat opposite her sister on the sofa. 'He has the patience of a saint.'

Maggie nodded, her mind straying to Sean for the squillionth time, even though she'd just spent half her day hating him. But then she already knew that all the varying emotions she felt for him were part and parcel of the one thing. She was mature enough to have known that fairly early on, even though admitting it out loud had been slower in coming.

Meanwhile Kath studied her face and a wave of sudden realisation hit her. 'Maggie, you have it too, don't you?'

Her sad eyes focused on the older sister whom she'd watched go to hell and back for three years. She just nodded again in silent answer.

Kath was off the sofa and in front of her on the footstool in the blink of an eye. 'They said there was a chance it was a hereditary thing but with Sinead and Ciara both sailing through their pregnancies it just never occurred to me that it might be true. How did you find out?'

'I've always had period problems, you know that.'

'But you *had* periods, though—I went for years with barely the sign of one.'

'Well, apparently it's still the same thing. The part of my body that deals out the fertility stuff is as out of whack as yours is, so my chances of conceiving naturally are next to none.'

'Oh, sweetie,' Kath reached a hand across to take Maggie's, her eyes welling, 'I'm sorry; I know how it feels to be told that. And I know how much you want a family.'

Maggie smiled a somewhat weak smile. 'Murphy's law, right? That's why I came up with the single-father plan. I can at least try to be a mother to kids who don't have one or who don't mind a second one that won't give them stepbrothers or sisters. And a guy who already has kids is more likely not to mind not having a baby again, right?'

Her hand was squeezed tightly. 'It makes more sense now. I just couldn't understand what you were thinking. But it all makes sense now.'

'See, there is method to my madness.'

Kath's mind worked on the new information for long moments and then she understood a little more. 'You're in love with Sean, though.'

Maggie flinched inwardly, her mind registering the fact that the words had been made a statement of fact rather than a question. Her eyes flickered downwards, hiding the emotional windows from her sibling, her voice dull. 'It doesn't really matter if I am.'

'That's why you've been so off with him—you're trying to push him away.'

'I have to.' She tugged her hand free and managed to glance at Kath's face for a split-second. 'I can't give him what he needs.'

'Because you can't have kids the old-fashioned way? Have you tried talking to him about it? You might find that it doesn't matter that much to him.'

'I can't do that…' her voice cracked on the words '…I can't make him go through all that, and he has a right to have kids of his own; he's the last male in his family—that stuff's important.'

'He said that?' Her eyes widened in surprise. 'How can he say that when there's every chance that even if he did have kids they might all be girls? It took his mother four attempts to have him!'

'I know that and he does too. But he'd still want to try, wouldn't he? And I can't do that.'

Kath leaned closer, her voice more determined. 'But you're not even giving him the option. How can he make a decision if he doesn't have all the facts?'

While Maggie battled to keep at bay the tears she'd held inside for a long time, Kath jumped in with another question. 'You know how he feels about you?'

Maggie's eyes moved upwards and locked with

Kath's. They locked and stayed put for a long, long time. And then she pushed herself up from the chair and walked towards the windows.

'You do, don't you? You know he's crazy about you.'

'I thought maybe we were headed that way, yes.'

Kath's breath caught. 'And yet you still won't tell him, or take a chance on him. Maggie, he has a right to know why you're pushing him away. If you love him then surely you should be prepared to give him the benefit of the doubt. He isn't like Tony.'

'How can you know that?' She swung around, the tears streaking down her cheeks. 'You can't tell me that he wouldn't end up exactly like him. Resenting every IVF treatment that didn't work, unable to cope with how I'd feel every time I found out I wasn't pregnant. I can't let him feel guilty for the rest of his life because he didn't love me enough. I can't put either of us through what you went through. It's better this way. And it's better that I do this now before whatever he feels is something serious.'

'You're not thinking straight.' Kath's voice calmed as she stood up and walked towards her sister. 'I was exactly the same. I used to think it would be better if Tony just left and found someone else. I even told him that towards the end. It was his decision to take my advice, no matter how much it killed me. You can't know that Sean will be the same. And to be honest I think you're selling him short.'

Maggie shook her head, her arms wrapping around

herself. 'It's too much to risk, Kath. I'm not as strong as you were. You were just so amazingly brave.'

'You think I was strong?' She stepped closer. 'Oh, honey, I wasn't strong, I was a mess. But Tony was never half as courageous as Sean O'Reilly. I'm sure that man has seen things we could only imagine in our worst nightmares. I'd bet my house on him being there for you.'

'I can't do it, Kath, I just can't. I'm better giving him up now and trying to find someone else I can love than being with him for a while and then losing him piece by piece.'

'You don't know that you would lose him.'

'And I don't know that I wouldn't. This way it's my choice.'

Kath sighed as she finally stood right in front of her, her hands reaching over to frame Maggie's tear-streaked face. 'Love doesn't just land in your lap every day, Maggie. It's a gift, a precious one. And sometimes you do have to fight a little harder for it. But it can be worth every battle. If you just give it a chance.'

'He's been through so much.' Her voice trembled on every word. 'Came home to make a life for himself with a little peace, with a family he could nurture—'

'Sean O'Reilly, super-stud, you used to call him.' She smiled.

'He went through dates like I go through bottled water when he first came back. But he didn't know what he wanted, he needs the right person as much as anyone does. Maybe a little more because he needs some beautiful memories to replace the bad ones he carries around.'

'He found her. You're the right one for him. Everyone can see it.'

Her head shook again, her arms unfolding so she could place her hands over Kath's where they rested on her face. 'No, Kath. Because I can't give him what he needs—'

'You don't *know* that, Maggie. Look at me; I haven't given up hope yet. I have Michael with me every step of the way and if it doesn't work out we'll adopt. There are kids out there without families that need one of their own. Plenty of them.'

'I know. But I want to give Sean the chance for a child that looks exactly like him, with those damn dark eyes of his and that stupid lop-sided smile. And the only way that can ever happen is if he's forced to look at someone else.'

'I think you're wrong.'

'It's my decision to make, though.' She unpeeled the hands from her face, took a deep breath and drew on the inner strength that she'd had to find in herself to keep going. It had taken some finding, had meant closing off a part of her heart forever. But it was what she had to do. Because she loved him that much.

Another deep, shuddering breath, and she looked her sister in the eye. 'You have to swear you won't tell him.'

Kath's face fell. 'I can't do that.'

'You have to.' Her voice got firmer. 'I mean it. If you tell him I'll never forgive you. You're my sister, Kath, my flesh and blood.'

A million emotions played across Kath's face. She understood Maggie's thinking, what she was going through. Because she'd been in a similar place for so long herself. She'd thought through every possibility, had wanted to try and make the best decisions for everyone, but in the end she'd failed. Maggie was just trying her own way to get through it. But that didn't mean that Kath thought she was right. She opened her mouth to speak. But Maggie's hands squeezed hers tightly.

'Please, Kath. Don't make me beg.'

Loyalty to family ran deep in their bloodlines and it won out over Kath's sense of what was right and wrong for two people she believed were made for each other.

'I promise.'

A small sob broke free and Maggie fell into her sister, her arms reaching out for the comfort of a hug. 'Thank you.'

CHAPTER ELEVEN

'HEY there.' Sean glanced up at Kath when she appeared in front of him at the main entrance to the house. 'You over seeing Maggie?'

'No, I was with her last night though. We had a long talk.'

His eyebrows rose. 'Really?'

'Yes, and now you and I need a talk.'

'She said something about me?'

'I can't answer that.'

'Then I don't see how we have too much to talk about.'

Kath stood her ground as he moved his box of groceries into one arm and dug deep in the pocket of his jeans for his keys before stepping past her to the door. With her back to him she looked skywards and then dived right on in. 'I'm not wrong about you two.'

Sean stared at his own reflection in the glass of the door. He waited a long moment and then asked in a low voice, 'About us two what?'

'About what I've known for a couple of months now.'

He continued looking in the glass. 'And that is?'

She swung round and glared at his reflection. 'Oh, you know what I'm talking about.'

'If she didn't talk about me last night then you still don't know anything for sure.'

'I knew it back then and I know it now. So what I want to know from you is what you plan on doing about it.'

'You're that convinced I should do something?'

'Yes!' Her arms rose at her side in frustration. 'I can't tell you why I know but I know and you need to just trust me on that. I'm trying to help.'

Sean stared into the glass for a long time, then he came to a decision, turning his head to look at Kath over his shoulder. 'You'd better come up.'

'Maggie can't see me.'

'She's not here, she had voice-overs to do at the station so she won't be back till later.'

Glancing over her shoulder regardless, Kath then stepped forward, 'Well, we better be quick, just in case.'

Inside his apartment Sean could see she was still on edge. She moved around the room, not quite pacing, because it wasn't in a straight line, but she couldn't stay still. Sean was no fool. He knew that whatever the conversation had been about it involved him in some form or she wouldn't be so determined. And his heart beat a little faster at the knowledge. He was no naïve, love-struck teenager but he had more faith now. Maggie wasn't immune to him.

'You should sit down—my floors won't take too much of that.'

'I haven't got time to sit down.'

'I told you it's safe; she won't be back for ages.'

'Can't we just be quick anyways?' Her eyes focused on his. 'You *are* going to do something, aren't you?'

Maybe it was time he trusted someone.

When he'd started to get closer to his new work colleague it hadn't been long before they'd started to mix with each other's families. Birthdays, holidays, births…so far, luckily, no funerals. Bonds had been formed similar to those of a married couple. Everything had just sort of fitted. Made sense.

And of all the bonds that had been made, Sean's with Maggie's sister had been one of the closer. He couldn't keep lying to her. She was just too like her younger sister for him to even try.

'I know.'

Kath stopped dead in her tracks and stared at him. 'You know what?'

'Why Maggie has been pushing me away and trying to find a single father to settle down with.'

'How *can* you know?'

His eyes avoided hers and he turned away to set his groceries on the counter top in the kitchen. 'I just do.'

'She's under the impression you don't.'

'I know, but I do.' Turning around, he leaned back against the counter and folded his arms across the front of his denim shirt.

Kath gaped at him. 'What did you do?'

A shrug. 'I made myself into what she thinks she's looking for.'

'You made yourself into a single-parent family?

How on earth did you…?' The penny dropped. 'You went on the site?' Then her brain worked a little and she gasped, 'You're the Romeo guy?'

He smiled slowly. 'Mentioned him, did she?'

'When we talked last night. After she told me everything we got on to the subject of her dates from the site. I think she was trying to let me see she believes she really can find someone else.' There was a pause and then she added, 'She really likes him. She's hoping to meet him soon. You know, she's never going to forgive you when she finds out it's you!'

Which was why he was determined she wouldn't find out. The secret would go to his grave if he had his way. Even if she strangled him trying to find out and *put* him in his grave.

'She's not going to meet him, and she's not going to find out.'

'I'm getting really sick of this with you two.'

He frowned. 'You don't have to get involved, Kath—'

'Oh, right, 'cos I should just stand here and watch the two of you be miserable for the rest of your lives!'

'I was going to say but I'm glad you have.' With two long strides he was in front of her and using his hands on her elbows to guide her back into a chair. Then his steady gaze fixed on her. 'Because I might never have found out what she was planning until I was invited to the damn wedding. Thanks to you I've had a chance to look at the possibilities.'

'You know how she feels about you, then?' Kath's face was incredulous. 'Then why have you been telling me I'm wrong? Why didn't you just do something?'

'I thought I knew she was interested. We'd been dancing around each other playing the flirting game for months. But then she just went cold on me and I started to have doubts. Being in love is apparently directly attached to a person's self-confidence levels.' He grimaced slightly. 'A survival thing, I'd guess.'

Her expression didn't change. 'And you're more confident now?'

'Hell, no. Now that I know the reason I'm…' he took up the pacing on her behalf, his hand reaching up to run back though his hair '…well, a little disappointed in her, I suppose. She should know me better. I would never walk out on someone I love just because the road is rocky. That's what I always believed real love was about.'

'In fairness you have been quite a jack the lad with the ladies.'

'Not for quite some time I haven't.'

There was a look of disbelief aimed at his pacing figure. 'Maggie told me you turned up at a restaurant with someone young enough to be your much younger sister.'

'That was so I could bump into Maggie and Paul.'

'Ah.'

'Yes, *ah*. It's about all I've managed so far. You know, disrupting her dates, being sarcastic about her choices, getting information by deceptive means. I'm a bit stumped as to what other dishonourable means I can use.' He stopped in front of her. 'I'm a hell of a guy really.'

'You love her.'

His mouth quirked upwards at the edges for a brief second. 'Yeah, that's a done deal.'

'Then maybe you should just try telling her every day till she caves in.'

It was a novel idea. His brain turned it over a few times and his smile gradually transformed into a wicked lop-sided grin. 'Are you suggesting in another roundabout way that I should try and seduce your sister?'

Kath answered the grin with one of her own. 'You know, I believe I am. Seduction of the heart rather than of the body, though. That's if you reckon you're up to it.'

'Well, maybe all those years as a jack the lad will have their uses.'

'Training.'

'Indeed.'

They continued grinning as the plan became more promising in each of their minds. Then Sean moved in front of her chair, leaned in and kissed her head. 'I like the way your mind works.'

'Let's just hope Maggie does.'

The voice-over had taken a lot longer than she'd thought it would. She had been tired all day and had put it down to the fact that she still ached from her mountain walk the day before. But then she had begun to cramp. And she'd known why she felt so bad. And knowing had only brought her pain of a different kind. The soul-destroying, heart-wrenching agony that came with knowing she would suffer the pain for no reason. Because her body just didn't work the way it was supposed to.

Her painkillers were at home so she only got worse on the trip back. She just wanted a couple of tablets, a hot-water bottle, her bed and a private place to weep. So the last thing she needed was to meet Sean on one of his insomnia walks.

She lifted her hand from her stomach and did her best to stand taller and not let him see her face.

'Voice-over done?'

'Yep, all done.' Her grin became a grimace as she turned her face from his and went through the door he held open.

He followed her. 'You eaten yet? Why don't you get cleaned up and come over for a late supper?'

'No, thanks, Sean.' She gripped the banister tight as another fierce cramp gripped her abdomen. 'Maybe some other time.'

'You got another date?'

'At this time of night?' She managed to force out a laugh but already there were stars around the edges of her vision. Just a couple of minutes and she'd be inside. Then he wouldn't have to see her and ask the questions that would inevitably come with seeing her in so much pain. 'I don't think so.'

Following closely behind her, he noticed how her steps became more faltering as she approached the last few stairs. She leaned towards the wall and his well-trained camera eyes caught sight of her white knuckles on the banister. 'Maggie?'

She felt the hallway sway.

'Maggie?' He jumped round her and looked down at her face, stunned by how pale she was. 'What the hell's wrong?'

Her smile was weak. She prayed he wouldn't be sweet to her. She couldn't take it if he was sweet. Sarcasm would have been more welcome, because she could have fought with that. At least for the final steps it would take to get to safety. But another cramp caught her and a moan escaped her mouth as she doubled up.

Sean swore savagely and immediately swept her forward into his arms. Taking a second to reposition her beside him, he helped her up the final step and along the hall. 'We need to get you to a doctor.'

'No, no doctor.' She leaned into him and allowed him to guide her to the door. 'I'll be all right when I get inside.'

'Like hell you will.'

'I will, honestly. I just need my painkillers.'

Painkillers? He started to panic and had to force himself to be calm. 'You have painkillers? For what exactly?'

Almost sighing with relief at the sight of her own front door, she tried to push away from him. 'It's a girl thing.' That should be enough to have him running screaming to his own apartment.

'OK, I get it.' He held her in a tight band of muscular arms and forced her key from her hand. 'Then let's get you inside and comfortable.'

'You really don't have to—'

'I know,' he smiled a warm smile at her, 'but I'm going to. So shut up for once in your life.'

Under the force of that amount of warmth, and due to her weakened state, she did as she was bid. She allowed him to guide her inside, heard the door slam when he kicked it closed, and then found herself helped into her bedroom. It was the one room in her place he hadn't been in and had she been more in charge she would have been completely unsettled by his being there. But seduction was hardly likely to be the first thing on his mind.

He set her on the edge of her bed and kneeled down in front of her to remove her shoes.

Maggie swallowed hard and asked in a weak voice, 'What are you doing?'

'I'm getting you comfortable.'

'You really don't have to do that.' She almost sighed when he held his hand around her ankle for longer than necessary. While his other hand slipped the shoe off, again slower than was probably necessary, she felt the fingers against her ankle caress before he set her foot down and moved to the other one. What else was he planning on removing to get her comfortable?

With the second shoe off his dark eyes swept up to lock with hers. He saw her wide-eyed expression and smiled a slow, lazy smile. 'The rest you can do on your own.'

It was only as she exhaled with a sharp burst of air that she realised she'd been holding her breath. 'That I can. Thanks.'

'No problem.' He stood up, towering over her. 'Now, where are your painkillers?'

'In the cupboard to the left of the cooker hood.'

'OK. You need anything else?' He continued smiling at her.

She really wished he wouldn't do that. He was just being so bloody nice. All he would need to do was add some affection and she'd yap all over him. That should be enough to add to the 'girl problem' for any sane male.

'A hot-water bottle helps.'

'No problem.' He reached a hand out and brushed her fringe back before adding, 'Get changed and I'll be right back.'

She sniffed when she reckoned he was out of earshot. Once she had her painkillers and hot-water bottle he had to go. He really did.

By the time he came back she had the most voluminous Victorian-style nightdress on that she could find. A Christmas present from her grandmother, it had lain in the bottom of her drawer for so long that it positively reeked of violet drawer-liners but it covered her entirely from head to toe.

She was curled on her side, foetal fashion, so he had to crouch down at the bedside to give her the tablets and a glass of water. Then he set the glass on her night stand and waved the hot-water bottle in front of her pale face. 'Where do you want this?'

She reached out a hand. 'I'll do it.'

He held it back from her reach. 'Where?'

Recognising the determination in his eyes and knowing fine well he wouldn't leave till she was comfortable, Maggie frowned and answered, 'My back.'

'Lower back?'

'Yes.' She squeezed the word out through gritted teeth as another cramp washed over her.

Fully expecting him to reach the bottle over her and tuck it against the covers, she was stunned when he stood up and moved around the bed. The mattress dipped behind her and she jumped as his hand moved the bottle beneath the covers and smoothed it down into place on her lower back. She forced her breathing to calm while he straightened the covers around her again and then gasped when she felt his body settle against hers, his arm snaking around her waist.

Oh, no. This couldn't happen.

CHAPTER TWELVE

'WHAT are you doing?'

He held her in place, his hand beginning to smooth in circles on her stomach through the covers. His deep voice sounded by her ear. 'My mum used to do this for my sister Erin when she got cramps. Erin swore by it.'

Despite the soothing heat from the hot-water bottle, Maggie's body tensed, which made the next cramp draw another low moan from her lips.

'Relax.' His hand continued to move in hypnotic circles. 'You bunch up like that it'll get worse.'

'You really don't—'

'Ssshhh. I'm going to stay with you till you fall asleep.'

If he stayed there was just no way she had a hope in hell of sleeping.

'Sean—'

'Ssshhh,' he whispered against her ear, 'don't make me sing you to sleep.'

She laughed. She'd heard his singing. It wasn't designed to soothe a troubled soul. 'Please don't do that.'

'Then relax.'

'How exactly am I supposed to do that while you're in bed with me?'

There was the briefest hesitation and then his deep voice answered with, 'You'll just have to try and forget all those fantasies you have about me.'

'Right.' *If only he knew.* When she'd first started to notice him as more than a workmate behind a camera she'd not gone much beyond accepting how easy he was on the eye. But then she had started to pay more attention to him when he was flirting with one of the many girlfriends he'd had in those early months. She'd wondered how she would react if he ever turned that charm on her. Had had several un-invited dreams that had shown her subconsciously that she was attracted to him.

Then, as the girlfriends had gradually faded out, he had begun to flirt with her and she'd responded in kind. It had been the beginning of the end. But all that had been before. Now was now. And she was just going to have to force herself to think calming thoughts.

For the first time in months she was almost thankful for the pain that reminded her of why she couldn't have her heart's very desire.

'For now anyway.'

What? She tried to focus on the softly whispered words. Surely he hadn't just said what she thought she'd heard?

He continued to move his hand, his voice rising a little. 'Is it this bad every time?'

'No.' Because there wasn't an 'every time'. That had been the first warning sign. She felt her throat closing.

'Can they do anything to make it less painful apart from give you the painkillers?'

Initially they'd told her that having a baby was the solution. She closed her eyes tight and shook her head against the pillow.

'You were like this when we did that piece on the ostrich farmers a few months back, weren't you?'

She'd told him at the time she'd had stomach flu. It had been the first time she had the pains since she'd found out. A sob built in her chest. She just wanted him to leave. Why did he have to pick *now* to be so damn tender?

'You could have told me. I'd have been there.'

Her voice was choked. 'You couldn't have done anything.'

'I could have been supportive. I could have made you rest, carried painkillers for you, rubbed your stomach till you felt better.'

The silent sob racked her body.

'That's what you do for someone you care about.' His voice was husky. 'You do what you can to help. You take some of the weight when that person needs you to.'

It was too much. Her whisper was tortured, her heart shredding into billions of tiny, irreparable pieces. 'Please go.'

His arm tightened. 'No.'

'Please, Sean.' It was a heartfelt plea as she turned her face into the pillow.

'No. I'm not going anywhere. You're stuck with me.'

Her silent sobs jerked her body against his and he held on to her. He didn't speak while she let it out and tears soaked her pillow. He didn't ask for an explanation, didn't stop his hand moving in soothing circles. He just stayed there. Until she stopped sobbing. Until her breathing evened out. And then he held her while she slept.

He wasn't going to let her go. Whether she liked it or not. Because she was his. And that was that.

'Oh, my God.' She groaned into her pillow when she woke up the next morning. Sean wasn't beside her but she had a sense that he'd been there for a long time.

And she'd cried her damned eyes out in his arms the night before. What the hell had she been thinking?

But that was the problem. She hadn't been thinking. She'd been feeling. And having held everything inside for so long it had been bound to spill out at some stage. She'd known it would—she wasn't superhuman. But she'd always planned that when it happened it would happen when she was alone. Not when Sean was holding her and saying things he could have had no idea would make it worse.

With another groan she shook her head and swung her legs over the edge of the bed. She glanced at her night stand, where the glass of water he'd brought her still sat, and she knew she should take painkillers again. It was often as bad the second day as the first.

Then she realised she smelt coffee. And toast. Her eyes widened; he was still here?

'Oh, my God.' She hid her face in her hands for several long moments, forcing herself to take deep breaths. Then she stood up and pulled a towelling robe over her ridiculous nightdress. A glance at her face in the mirror made her grimace. But she wasn't about to take the time to freshen up. In fact the less attractive the better as far as she was concerned. She had an eviction to do.

Sean had lain beside her, watching her sleep until he couldn't take it any more. He had wanted to hold her until her eyes opened. So that he was the first thing she saw. But he just couldn't trust himself not to tell her there and then how he felt. That was a battle yet to come.

When she eventually appeared from the bedroom she was still pale, but a tinge of red touched her cheeks.

'Good morning. How are you feeling?'

'Better, thank you.' She stood a safe distance away from his dark, direct stare. 'I can take it from here.'

'I made you some breakfast. Those painkillers can't be good for your stomach.' He turned his back to her and poured tea into a mug. 'Do you need to take more of them?'

She looked at him with narrowed eyes as he turned and moved towards her with the mug. Instinctively she moved back a step.

Sean noticed the movement and he frowned in annoyance. He set the mug down on the counter roughly halfway between them and then loaded bread into the toaster. 'You need to eat before you do.'

'I know.' She frowned back at him. 'Really, you can go now, I'll be fine.'

He watched from the corner of his eye until she stepped closer to collect her mug and then he moved. His hand shot out, and in the blink of an eye had captured her wrist. The quick movement caught her off guard so he used her momentary hesitation to his advantage and tugged her closer. When she was by his side he leaned his face close to hers.

His eyes searched hers, then he smiled a slow, purely sensual smile. 'This isn't how this is going to go with us any more, Mary Margaret.'

'What isn't?' She willed herself to look away from his eyes. *Do it, Maggie, look away.*

'This stepping away, sniping at each other and not talking game.'

'Is that what we're doing?' *Go on, Maggie, look away. Stamp on his foot or something.*

'I think you know it is. But it's done. Enough.'

She swallowed. 'I'm not stepping away from you, I'm just saying I'm fine right now and you don't need to babysit me any more.' *Look away!*

'I'm staying put.'

'Indefinitely?'

'Is that an offer?'

What? She couldn't look away or she wouldn't have been able to search his eyes for some hint of a teasing light. That was the second innuendo he'd made, unless her memory from the night before served her wrong. He couldn't possibly…

While he quirked an eyebrow in question her eyes widened. Oh, no. She couldn't allow him to make a pass at her, *not now*! Not when she'd spent so long doing exactly what he'd just accused her of. Stepping away from him.

She could handle her feelings for him so long as he was at arm's length.

'Sean—'

'Yes?'

'I don't want you to think that I don't appreciate what you did last night—'

'You were in pain.'

In more ways than he could ever know. 'Yes, I was, but I'm fine now.'

'Are you?'

Any moment now she was going to look away from those dark eyes. Any moment. 'I'm fine.'

The dark eyes blinked, black lashes brushing against his tanned skin. Then he shook his head. 'I don't think so.' He kept on looking at her. 'So I'm not going away.'

'Why are you being like this?'

His thumb grazed over the pulse that beat hard in her wrist and he smiled. 'It's called caring about someone.'

'I know you care. You don't need to be my nurse-maid for me to know that.'

'Stop pushing me away, Maggie; I'm not going.' He stared at her for a long moment, his smile still in place. Then, just like that, he released her and turned away.

Maggie watched with suspicious eyes as he removed toast, buttered it, lifted his mug and moved into the living room to sit down.

She knew when he dug his heels in he was an immovable force. But she had never planned on having that immovable force dug in, in her own living room. Her mind sought frantically for some way to get him to leave. Reasoning that she felt better hadn't worked. And, truth be told, she hadn't even thought about how she was feeling since she'd walked into the kitchen.

He was determined to be supportive, to be her best friend in his own inimitable way. But the longer he remained, the longer he continued to be supportive and affectionate and, damn him, *sweet*, the harder it would get for her to follow through on what she knew was the right thing to do. She wasn't strong enough for that.

Then an idea occurred to her. Maybe if she actually enlisted his help in her search for someone who measured up to him, he would see that she was serious. If she fell for someone in front of him he would have to see that there wasn't any point in hanging around.

It shouldn't be so very difficult. After all, it wasn't as if he'd even made a pass at her at any stage. And surely someone who was really in love would have done that by now?

It made perfect sense. And gave her a boost of

confidence so that by the time she joined him in the living room she even managed a smile.

'I do appreciate what you're doing.'

'I should think so,' he answered her with a mouthful of toast and the hint of a smile. 'I'm a hell of a guy.'

'Yes, you've mentioned that.'

He swallowed the food and broadened his smile to a familiar leery grin. 'Well, maybe you should pay more attention.'

'OK, then, I accept your offer of help,' she smiled sweetly, 'from the *other* night. Because I'm feeling fine right now, I really am. So you can help me with finding a better husband candidate.'

A slice of toast hovered briefly in front of his mouth. Then he shrugged. 'OK. You eat some breakfast, have a shower and we'll spend the day at it.'

'Great.' She grinned warmly at him.

He'd soon give up. She'd make him see she was serious. Because she had to get him to back off. She just couldn't deal with him being so close.

CHAPTER THIRTEEN

'NOT that one.'

Maggie scowled at him where he sat so close that his shoulder almost touched hers. 'What's wrong with him? He's cute.'

Sean grimaced. 'Cute? You could get married to the easter bunny if cute is what you're looking for. Next.'

'No, hang on. You're supposed to be helping here. Not dismissing everyone because they have one teeny thing wrong with them.'

'One teeny thing? The last one still lives with his mother.'

'Because he needs someone to look after his son while he's at work.'

'And she'll stay there to keep doing that so you can keep working too. It's a no go.'

'I'd work less.'

He stared at her, the surprise showing on his face. 'You're going to quit work?'

'Not quit exactly, just do less hours. I've been thinking about it for a while.' She shrugged, as if by doing so they could just brush past something that was so major.

It wasn't happening, though. 'You can't give up

everything, Maggie. A big part of who you are is what you do. And you love your work.'

'But it can't be everything.'

'I know that—'

'Yes, you of all people know that,' she nudged his shoulder with her own, 'because you gave up award-winning work to come home.'

'That was different. I haven't quit on what I do, I've just changed the direction some. And I quit as much because I hadn't the stomach for it any more as for a need to come home. I can't completely change who I am, it's just in me.'

'I understand that.'

'I'm glad you do. Just think things through a bit more before you make any major decisions.' He glanced at her, then back at the screen. 'Next guy.'

She ignored the last demand. Instead she turned her chair an inch so she could study the face lit by the glow from her computer screen. 'Do you regret making changes?'

'No,' the answer was quick and determined as he turned his eyes to hers, 'I'm where I want to be. I did what I could but I could have spent my whole life there watching people destroy lives rather than coming back to try and build something for myself. If people don't try for the things that matter then the world will end up a pretty damn horrible place. *I know*.'

'That's what I want, to build something.'

'I know.' His voice was soft.

Her heart reached out for him, forcing the words from her lips, 'It's what I want for you, too.'

'I know.'

She had to force herself to look away from the warmth in his eyes. It just never got any easier though.

He reached out a hand and turned her face to his with gentle fingertips on her chin. Then he waited until her long lashes rose and she looked him in the eye, her pupils enlarging for a split-second. And he smiled. 'We'll get there, Maggie. You wait and see. I may not agree with the idea of you giving up full-time work and landing me with some wannabe teenage reporter but if a change of direction is what you decide then I'll support it. Just like I'd expect you to let me make any decisions for myself.'

'You're thinking of making some decisions?' Her voice came out a little breathless.

'Could be,' his fingers moved across her chin before he let go, 'but don't you worry. We'll talk about anything I decide in good time. Right now we're trying to find what you're looking for. Maybe we should widen the search.'

The reporter in her remained curious. 'What kind of decisions?'

As he leaned a little closer his fingers reached out for the keyboard and he scrolled down to the next profile. 'Maybe I've decided to settle down myself. I could have a look-see on this site of yours.'

Having him help her find a partner was one thing, but apparently the idea of seeking one for himself was something different. 'Whatever happened to ladies first?'

He smiled at the screen. 'Come on, fair's fair. We could go on a double date.'

The very thought made her feel physically sick. 'I don't think so.'

'Aw, c'mon, it would be fun.' He turned to look at her. 'We're friends, it makes sense that we try for partners who wouldn't interfere with that. This way we can make sure we all get on.'

She gaped at him.

'Unless part of the many changes you're planning on making includes me out of your life completely.'

'No, not completely.' It was certainly what she'd hoped for when she'd first decided to let him go romantically. But she hadn't actually considered how she'd feel seeing him with someone else. If it hurt to see as much as it hurt to think about, it might be tough for her to stay being his friend.

'But you didn't think we'd see as much of each other, did you?'

'No, I guess not. But that happens when friends get married and their lives change. It's just a natural progression.' With one piece of honesty came a need to make amends of some kind or another, despite the fact that his face remained devoid of emotion. That damned self-control of his. 'It doesn't mean I'd stop caring. Even if we didn't spend as much time together.'

His eyes searched hers long and hard, then his voice came out with a husky note. 'I'd miss us.'

Maggie felt a physical pain so sharp in her chest that she almost gasped as the words spilled out. 'Me too.'

He allowed the moment to pass with an affectionate smile and then spoke words that knocked her further off kilter. 'Tell me what your heart desires, Mary Margaret, and I'll find it for you.'

What her heart desired her heart couldn't have. Under his steady gaze she faltered. Maybe the idea of getting him to see she was serious about her search for a husband, so he would realise she wouldn't change her mind, wasn't such a good one after all. She should have moved away from him months ago, sold her apartment, changed jobs, moved halfway across the world. Not allowed him the opportunity to sit within touching distance and ask her to name her heart's desire.

His shoulder nudged hers. 'Come on, then.'

She cleared her throat. 'You first.'

'What happened to ladies first?'

'I'm a modern, independent woman, I can deal with it.'

'OK, then.' With a forward shove of his chair he inched nearer to the keyboard and leaned close to her again to fill in the search bar.

'Let's see, we'll go with twenty-eight to thirty-five.' He pursed his lips together and moved his head from side to side as he typed. 'Auburn-haired, I think.'

Auburn-haired? She swallowed and asked, 'Gone off the student type now, have we?'

'Someone with a little more life experience would
be better I think.' It hadn't been unnoticed by him
that she'd brushed over the hair colour, so he continued, 'Let's go with…I dunno…' his head moved
from side to side again '…five six to five eight. Slim
build.'

Maggie sat her five-feet-eight frame a little taller
in her chair and frowned at the screen. 'Something
against tall women now?'

'I don't want to end up with a bad back. But I
guess it wouldn't matter lying down.' He turned and
winked at her. 'A little taller would be OK, though.'

She scowled as he looked back at the screen.

'Job doesn't matter, has kids doesn't matter, wants
kids doesn't matter—'

'How can you say "wants kids doesn't matter"?'

'It doesn't matter at the dating stage.'

'But you're not being honest, are you?'

'I think that wanting children is a bridge that
should be crossed whenever you know you've found
the right one. It doesn't matter if they want a million
kids if you don't have something really strong first,'
he turned his eyes on her, 'don't you think?'

What he said did make sense. 'But by talking
about it up front then no one is under any illusions.
To get involved with someone, learn to care for them
and then find out they don't want a family would
only end up in heartache.'

'So honesty is the best policy.'

She could only stand to have him look her in the
eye for another brief second before she pushed her

chair back and walked towards the kitchen. 'It's a good idea.'

'So you don't think I should just try getting to know someone a bit first and then sound them out?'

'You could do that if you wanted to.'

The fake uninterest injected into her voice didn't escape him. 'I guess if they had kids already then there wouldn't be so much of an issue.'

She had got as far as the centre of the kitchen when he finished. Immediately she swung round and stared at him with glittering eyes. 'What exactly are you hinting at?'

'I wasn't aware I was hinting at anything.'

'Like hell you weren't.'

He leaned back from the keyboard, turned his chair towards her and folded his arms across his chest. 'Since you seem to know, why don't *you* tell me? What exactly am I hinting at?'

Her eyes widened as her anger grew. Her gut instinct was telling her *he knew*, but if he knew then why wouldn't he just come right out and say so? And if he knew, how could he know unless Kath had told him? She found it hard to believe her sister would break so great a confidence. So what *did* he know? And what could she say without giving herself away?

Pacing gave her a few moments to think.

He hadn't been happy with her dating method from the start. So what if it was that he was getting at? That made more sense to her than believing her sister would tell him her secret.

She stopped pacing. 'You think I lie to these guys?

That's why you think I've not had any success with them?'

'Is it? Or is it just that you haven't been honest about what it is you're looking for?'

'You think I'm not being honest with *myself*?'

'Are you?'

'You could stop answering every one of my questions with another question any time and that would be helpful!'

Unfolding his arms from across his chest, he leaned forward and rested his elbows on his knees, his eyes steady on hers. 'All I'm doing is trying to be helpful. You may need to rethink the way you're going about finding the right guy for you. 'Cos let's face facts here, up till now you've not been doin' so great. And if a little more honesty helps then why fight it?'

'And that's what this is about?'

He smiled softly. 'Now who's answering a question with a question?'

'You really want me to find the right one?'

He nodded. 'Absolutely.'

She wasn't entirely sure she believed him. But she *wanted* to believe him. Any alternative would lead to a betrayal that would hurt beyond words and an emotional battle she wasn't up to fighting.

'OK. Then let's get to it.'

He pushed his chair back as she walked towards him, making a space for her by his side.

'So, let's restart this search, then.'

His hand stopped hers from reaching the keyboard. 'No, we're still doing mine. Then we'll do yours.'

Maggie glared at him. 'You don't want to find someone on here—you can get dates by just breathing in and out. This is what *I* want, remember?'

He held on to her hand and leaned in close enough to smell her hair. He loved that scent. Then he smiled a slow, sensual smile. 'This isn't all about what you want any more. It's about what I want too.'

'And you want an internet date?'

'What's sauce for the goose, Mary Margaret. We have a double date to set up.'

CHAPTER FOURTEEN

HER date was gorgeous. Male-model material. There was barely a female in the room who hadn't turned to look at him when they walked in the room. And he was a very funny, smart, sexy kind of a guy. Everything she could possibly have wanted. He had a successful career as a property developer, two small children from the marriage that had only ended when his wife had run off with her personal trainer and he was keen to find someone to love again. He was an all-round pretty great candidate.

Trouble was, Maggie couldn't seem to concentrate on him while Sean was sitting across from them with his own pretty great candidate. She would be ideal for him; they made a gorgeous couple and they got on so well an outsider would have thought they'd known each other for years. Maggie was jealous as hell.

'Would you like to dance?'

She forced herself to look into Gavin's blue eyes. Maybe if they'd been a rich dark brown filled with secrets and hopes and genuine affection she could have held his gaze for longer. But instead she glanced away fairly quickly.

'So, would you?'

She found herself looking across at Sean and the

lovely Terri while they both laughed at something Sean had just said. She wanted to be in on the joke. She wanted him just for a second to look at her and smile.

She was the most unreasonable woman on the planet.

'I'm sorry, Gavin.' She turned a broad smile on him. 'What did you say?'

He smiled back at her, his perfect, even white teeth glinting at her in the candlelight. 'I was wondering if you'd like to dance.'

They had retired to the lounge of the intimate country hotel near Strangford Lough after dinner, the sound of the country and western band eventually too much for them to ignore. But Maggie hadn't actually planned on being one half of the first couple to brave the dance floor.

She looked around the room at the people sitting quite happily at their tables. 'Maybe when there are more dancers?'

He laughed. 'Are you shy?'

'Not usually.' She laughed along with him. 'I have people look at me a lot but I guess I'm not used to being the floor show.'

'I'll look out for you.' He reached a hand out to her, palm upwards.

She looked down at the large hand, then glanced over at Sean again. He had leaned in to whisper something in Terri's ear, damn him. Right, that was *it*; she was going to have a good time with Gavin if it killed her.

Her hand settled on Gavin's and she smiled sweetly at him. 'I believe you will.'

Somewhere in her mind she recognised the fact that her hand didn't feel as right there as it did when it was enclosed in Sean's. And somewhere else in her mind she truly resented Sean for that fact.

The second thought meant it wasn't completely accidental that she managed to kick Sean in the shin as she got up from the table. 'Oops, clumsy me.'

Sean smiled as he reached a hand under the table to rub his leg. 'No worries, I have another one.'

Terri laughed and inched closer to his side and Maggie had to grit her teeth as she walked away. She should have said a more determined 'no' to the double-date idea.

On the way to the dance floor several people looked at them and smiled. Several women smiled a little more than necessary at Gavin as far as Maggie was concerned. In her damned overactive mind she had to admit that he was possibly a little too good-looking for his own good.

The band was gracious enough to change to an upbeat waltz by the time they got to their destination, and Gavin swung her into his arms *á la* Fred Astaire. It should have been perfect as she smiled up into his handsome face. If Sean hadn't dramatically limped to their sides with Terri, still laughing, at his heels.

'Fancy meeting you guys here.'

'Funny, that.' She glared at him and then smiled a larger smile at Gavin. 'You dance very well.'

'Anything to impress a gorgeous girl.' He spun them round in a circle. 'So, is it working?'

'You're doing OK.' She laughed and patted him on the shoulder.

'Good, 'cos,' he leaned his head towards her ear, 'you just happen to be a gorgeous girl.'

They were bumped to one side.

'Crowded on here, isn't it?'

Maggie glared at Sean.

He grinned. 'Swap.' And swung Terri at Gavin as he grabbed hold of Maggie's arm.

Neither Gavin nor Terri complained about the move as Sean spun them away and out of earshot.

'What the hell are you doing?' She smiled through gritted teeth.

'I thought it was time for a team meeting.'

'A team meeting? Now we're a team?'

'We've always been a team.' He pulled her closer to the length of his body and swayed her from side to side. 'So, how's your date going?'

Maggie tried to ignore the shiver of pleasure that ran down her spine when his breath tickled against the sensitive skin beneath her ear. She sighed. Oh, well, at least when she was being held so close she didn't have the problem of not being able to look away from his eyes.

'It's going great; yours?' As if she damn well had to ask. She'd witnessed first-hand how fantastically wonderful his date had been so far.

'She's gorgeous.'

'Yes, she is.' She rolled her eyes over his shoulder.

'And she thinks my jokes are funny.'

'We all know you're just hilarious.'

'She's smart.'

'Super.'

He leaned his head back to look at her face and smiled an irresistible lop-sided smile. 'Yeah, that's exactly the word for her. *Super.* Didn't I say the picking dates for each other thing would be a good idea?'

She quirked an eyebrow and answered with more than a hint of sarcasm, 'Is that what we did? I must have missed the part where I got to choose your date, being distracted as I was by the sight of you drooling all over my computer.'

'I picked a good one for you, though. Admit it.'

Yes, he had. In fact, his enthusiasm for picking her a great date had been the one thing that had allayed her fears about his knowing anything that he shouldn't. So why wasn't she drooling all over Gavin the same way Sean was over Terri? Was it quite simply that Sean wasn't as attached to her as she was to him?

The idea should have brought her some sense of relief at her deception. But it didn't. It just made her feel empty.

'He's a nice guy.'

Sean grimaced. 'Ouch. Insult him, why don't you?'

And there were those eyes again. Only this time they were sparkling at her. She laughed, despite how annoyed she wanted to remain with him. 'There's absolutely nothing wrong with being nice. You should try it some time.'

The band his arm was creating around her waist tightened. 'I try it every day. You just hate the fact that I picked a good 'un this time.'

'A good 'un?' She laughed again. 'And what exactly is that?'

'A good guy, a great date. A candidate in any single woman's book. What's wrong with him?'

He's not you. While they smiled at each other the truth was only too obvious to her. Again and again it all came back to Sean. To the one thing her heart desired that she just couldn't allow herself to be selfish enough to have. Because he deserved so much more than she was capable of giving him.

She managed to look away, her eyes straying back towards their 'dates'. 'There's nothing wrong with him. Apart from the fact he's currently hitting on your date.'

Sean looked across. 'Damn. So he is. I'd better go rescue her, then.'

'You're such a hero.'

'I know.' He waited until she looked back at him and then winked. 'It's just a shame the woman of my dreams doesn't seem to notice that right now.'

Maggie swallowed hard, her jealous streak kicking in so hard she almost groaned with the pain of it. 'Maybe she will if you go on over and rescue her.'

'Right, well I'll go rescue poor Terri, then.'

Unconsciously running her hand over his broad

back, she focused her eyes momentarily on his mouth. 'I'll help.'

He leaned down and brushed a light kiss on her lips with the mouth she'd just looked at. Then his arm squeezed again as he looked down at her stunned expression. 'You're a real pal.'

Maggie stood rooted to the ground while he walked over and politely removed Terri from Gavin and back into his arms. It took all of her on-camera skills to muster a smile as her date then returned to her side. 'Shall we?'

'I think I need a drink actually.'

'Your wish is my command.'

With a final glance at Sean as he pulled Terri closer she turned and left the dance floor. She needed a *large* drink. And a tub of very fattening ice cream. And chocolate. Anything that might numb her lips and take the memory of a brief kiss from her mind.

Sean smiled inside and out while he whisked Terri around the dance floor after Maggie left it. He was more optimistic than he'd been in a long time. More alive than he'd felt in a lifetime. The fight for Maggie was certainly not easy but it was invigorating as all hell.

'You look very pleased with yourself.'

'Do I?' He twirled Terri again for good measure. 'Must be because I have such a very excellent dance partner.'

'You really are a charmer, you know.'

'Yeah, I know.'

'And you really are crazy about that friend of yours.'

Glancing down, he had the good grace to look sheepish. 'Not doing so well at hiding it, then. It's that obvious, huh?'

'Only to the trained eye.' Terri laughed and leaned forward to sweep a kiss across his cheek. 'And this trained eye says you're not alone in the whole crazy thing. How long has Maggie been fighting you off?'

'A while.'

'And yet you keep coming back for more?'

'You gotta do what you gotta do.' He shrugged. 'She's worth it. She's just not thinking too straight right now.'

'You're that certain you can win her over?'

'No. Yes. I hope so.'

'How do you keep going?'

He leaned close to her ear as the music got louder and couples began to join them on the dance floor. 'I'm not quite sure, but if there's one thing I learnt in my time away from home it's that things that really matter are worth fighting for.'

Standing on her toes, she asked him up close, 'Even if you don't win in the end?'

'I won't spend the rest of my life knowing I let her go without one hell of a fight. No matter what happens.'

The smile started small and then, piece by piece, transformed into an affectionate grin. 'Sometimes I wish we'd made it, you and me.'

He answered her kiss on the cheek with one of his

own and then looked down into her eyes. 'We were too young.'

'I know. Everything turns out the way it's supposed to.'

'I really appreciate this, Terri.'

'You'd better—I had major persuading to do with Gavin to get him to put those profiles up on the site, even for forty-eight hours. And you'd better hope that this wasn't too devious a stunt, even for you.'

He grimaced. 'I will admit to a little guilt now that we're here. But I'll try anything if it works in the end.'

'Good luck.' She jerked her head in the direction of their table. 'Now can we go back so I can keep an eye on my husband?'

'So are you seeing the lovely Terri again?'

'Probably.' Sean smiled from the driver's seat. 'What about you and Gavin?'

'He didn't even ask for a kiss goodnight, so I'd say that's a "no".'

'Well, damn, that wasn't *polite*.'

She laughed. 'No, it wasn't.' The fact that Sean hadn't kissed Terri goodnight had cheered her up immensely. Well, that and several glasses of a rather good dry white wine. But the no-kissing thing was definitely in the lead.

'Maybe he's a second-date-kiss kinda guy.'

'We'll never know.'

He risked a sidelong glance at her. 'Not what your heart desires, then?'

'No, not what my heart desires.' She sighed and sank deeper into the seat, her humour dissipating. 'I'm thinking of quitting.'

'Quitting what?'

'The big search. I'm just going to stay single.'

'Forever?'

'I think so.' She turned her face to the side-window and watched as he made the turn to the house. 'I'm just not cut out for it.'

'That's ridiculous; of course you're cut out for it. Whatever "it" is.' He reached a hand across and enfolded his fingers around hers. 'Tell me what you want, Maggie.'

'I want what doesn't exist—' she cursed the wine for loosening her tongue, and her heart for immediately sensing how right her hand was in his '—happily-ever-after and a magical world.'

'And you think that's not possible. *I* still want to believe.'

'You of all people?'

He smiled as he made the final turn. 'Me of all people. Because if I don't then what is there?'

Maggie had never been more pleased to see the house. She needed to be out of the car. She needed to be inside so she could eat ice cream and possibly cry some more. The night had suddenly depressed her beyond reason or calorie-counting. And this conversation wasn't helping.

He squeezed her hand before letting it go, stopping the car and pulling up the handbrake. Then he halted her hand on the seat-belt release and waited for her to look up at him in the dim light from the dashboard. 'Wait.'

She blinked up at his shadowed face.

'Where did your fight go, Mary Margaret?'

'I used it up on a tonne of useless internet dates.'

His teeth glinted as he smiled. 'I keep telling you, you just keep looking at the wrong ones.'

'You picked this one and all that happened was he kept looking sideways at *your* date.'

'My date was super, remember?'

'Oh, I remember.' She pushed the release, pulled her hand from his and got out of the car.

Sean caught up with her inside three strides. 'So double-dating doesn't work for us.'

'No, that much we've established.'

'And you're done with the internet dates.'

'Yep.' She kept on walking.

They were under the porch light by the time he grasped her arm and tugged her around. 'You can't quit, Maggie.'

Her eyes widened. 'Why can't I?'

'It's there for you. You just need to trust yourself.'

Her mouth went dry. And she was stuck staring into his eyes again.

His smile was slow, sensual, dangerous. 'I did say I wouldn't ask permission.'

And with that he hauled her forward and kissed her.

CHAPTER FIFTEEN

SHE'D dreamed about this very moment for so long. It was exactly what her heart had desired. But it was still what she couldn't have.

He drew her closer to the length of his hard body, moved his mouth against hers and drew her exhaled breath into his lungs.

It was what she couldn't have. But she wanted it. Lord, she wanted it so badly.

She was going to have to push him away. Because allowing them to get this close was the very opposite of what she'd been trying to do. But apparently when a person's heart's desire was presented to them it wasn't easy to let go. She'd just take a minute. A little minute. And then she'd make him stop.

His mouth moved in slow, confident sweeps across hers while his hands moved over her back in firm strokes. He teased, tasted, silently asked for her surrender.

Somewhere in the blurred distance Maggie heard a moan. *Her own?* Oh, lord. Just another minute. Then she'd let go.

He increased the pressure of lips and hands, his tongue moved over her mouth, sought entry and was rewarded. And another moan sounded in the air around them. *His.*

One more minute. She wriggled to get her hands closer to his chest, telling herself it was so she could push him away. But instead her disobedient fingers tangled in his shirt and she held on. Her breathing became laboured, her heart beating so loudly in her chest that she couldn't hear anything else. *In a minute.*

He dragged his mouth from hers, his breath fanning across her swollen lips as he whispered her name. 'Maggie.'

She couldn't speak. His hands moved to the small of her back, pushed upwards beneath the edge of her top, touched fingertips against naked skin. And without thought she dropped back her head, inviting his mouth to the long length of her neck. She had to stop this. She really did.

His tongue ran along her neck, his lips showering her sensitive skin with kisses as light as the beat of a butterfly's wings.

'Sean…' She exhaled his name, inhaled it on a gasp. 'Sean.'

'Ssshhh.' The sound tickled against her damp skin, causing goose-pimples. 'Don't speak.'

She had to speak. 'We can't do this.'

'Yes, we can.' His hands moved up and down on her back.

'*I* can't do this.'

'Yes, you can.' He kissed the pulse below her ear.

The fists tangled in his shirt tightened for a brief second. 'I can't.'

He didn't stop kissing or touching. 'Tell me why.'

'I can't.' She felt a sob build low in her chest.

'Yes, you can Maggie, you can tell me.'

'No.' The word escaped with the sob and she finally found the will to uncurl her fingers and push against his chest. She moved her head from side to side to escape the ravages of his mouth. *'Please.'*

His mouth stilled. He moved his hands from her skin, smoothed her blouse into place, but didn't let her go. Instead he moved his head away from her neck, his eyes downcast while he spoke. 'I won't go away.'

Her chest rose and fell with her laboured breathing. 'Sean…'

When his head rose his eyes were as dark as the night sky beyond the halo of the porch light. He searched her eyes for a long moment. 'Go ahead and try telling me you don't want this.'

'I don't.'

'Liar.' He smiled. 'You may be able to lie but your body doesn't do it so well.'

'Why are you doing this?'

'You know why.'

She swallowed hard. 'I do?'

'Yes, you do.' His hands caressed against the material of her top again, his voice low and hypnotic. 'Just have a bit of a think about it for a minute.'

She was going to end up crying in his arms again. No amount of blinking was holding the tears. Because she knew what he was telling her. Knew it, wanted it and was going to have to reject it.

'I don't need to think.' She shook her head and

tried to get free of his hold. 'I don't want this from you; I've never asked for it.'

He frowned and held her in place. 'No, but you've got it. And I'm not going away.'

'You have to. I'm telling you I don't want this from you.' Her eyes welled.

'Tell me why.'

Her voice rose as the tears spilled over. 'If I do, will you go away?'

'Only if it's a good enough reason for me to go,' his eyes followed the tracks of the tears along her cheeks, 'and it would need to be good.'

'Let me go.'

He shook his head.

'I mean right now this minute,' she took a deep, if somewhat shaky breath and raised her hands from his chest to brush at her cheeks, 'then we'll talk.'

'I warn you, if you make a run for your apartment I'll beat you there.'

'I won't run.' She'd been running from doing this for a long time. But now she didn't have a choice. He'd forced her into a corner, and the only way out of that corner was to take the hard route. The truth. She'd tried to make it easy by pushing him away and that hadn't worked.

He seemed to think for a long time, then his hands moved from her back and he watched as she stepped away from him. He watched as she swiped at her cheeks again and avoided looking directly at him. And he felt a sense of deep foreboding. This was going to be tough. Maggie had had her mind made up about this for months.

With a silent breath he stood a little taller. 'OK, I'm listening.'

'I can't be with you, not like this.'

'Why not?'

'Because I love you too much.'

He smiled affectionately at her. 'I don't follow.'

'You deserve someone who can give you a wonderful life,' her voice shook and she had to take another breath to steady it, 'someone who can help you make a tonne of good memories to overshadow all the bad ones you have.'

'We can do that.'

The soft tone of his voice drove her over the edge, her eyes flashing with anger when she looked up at him. 'No, we can't. Because I can't give you a family!'

'And my having a family is what will make me happy? Being with you wouldn't be enough?'

'No, it wouldn't!' Her voice rose. 'Not after time. I want a family, Sean, you know that. It's what I've wanted ever since I was old enough to know what family meant. The fact that I know I can't have one is like living every day already being dead. Can you honestly say that you want to feel that way?'

'I already know how that feels.'

His words stopped her tirade. 'How could you?'

His smile disappeared, he fidgeted the briefest amount, but he still managed to look her in the eye. 'I was dead for years. Because if I wasn't dead inside it meant I had to feel and that would have hurt too much.'

Maggie couldn't move. All she could do was stand in the one place and stare at him. Listening to him while his voice came out on a dull monotone.

'I was going to go out there to do a job. It was what I'd wanted to do ever since I worked out how to use a camera and war correspondents were my heroes. What they did was heroic to me: they went from war to war and they sent back reports that held the rest of the world riveted to their TV screens.' He took another breath, ran a hand through his hair, his chin dropping for a second and then rising so his eyes could meet hers again. 'But I didn't know what it cost them. You want to talk about dying inside, Maggie, we'll talk about it.'

'You don't need to—'

His frustration at holding back from her, at trying to out-think her, at having to be so devious to stop her from doing what she was set on doing, all over-flowed into anger. He stepped towards her, eyes flashing in warning. 'Because if you're going to push me out of your life when we have something this important then I'm going to fight you every step of the way. And that means you understanding why I'm fighting that hard.'

'Sean—' she shook her head '—please don't do this.'

'I came home because I just couldn't do it any more. It was poisoning my soul. I thought by running away I might learn what it was to feel again. And I did learn, when I met you.' He shook his head. 'Go right on ahead, stand there and tell me that all the time we've spent together means nothing to you. Tell me that this wasn't supposed to happen.'

'I can't, but I still can't let this happen.' She shook her head, more frantically this time. Then she tried to step past him.

He caught her arm in a tight grip. 'Don't do this. I need you and, whether you'll let yourself admit it or not, you need me.'

It was too much to deal with his raw emotion as well as her own. She felt a chill run right down her spine as she wrenched her arm free, her eyes staring blankly at the door. 'I need you to let me go, Sean. Because I've already let go. I want you to have someone who can give you the fairy tale. Bring magic into your life. And I can't do that. So there's no point in breaking each other's hearts.'

'You've already brought me a fairy tale.' He watched as she turned her eyes to his and his heart hit his feet. He'd never seen that look before, not in Maggie's eyes. She'd gone blank, every spark gone from the depths of green. And it took that look for him to realise that he might already have lost her, even before he'd started chasing. 'You woke me up with laughter first, then you were the first person to make me talk and trust. With you as a friend I rediscovered all the good stuff that comes from having friends and a family.'

'The kind of a family that you can't have with me.'

'You don't know that.'

'I saw what it did to Kath, all those years of trying. It killed her marriage, killed the magic that she had in her life. And I won't do that to us.'

He frowned at her reasoning. 'So you're just going to kill it yourself. Is it really that hard to believe we could get through it? Damn it, Maggie, do you really have that little faith in me?'

'I'm right about this, you'll realise it one day.'

He swore loudly, shook his head in disbelief and leaned towards her with eyes that sparked dangerously. 'Oh, you're a piece of work. You just stand there and make all the decisions; you don't even care about my feelings enough to talk this through.' He laughed cruelly. 'You've looked at this from every angle and come up with one of those great Maggie Sullivan schemes to right the world. And all the way through this great decision you've never once believed in me enough to know that I'd have stood by you no matter how tough it got.'

His reasoning went straight from her ears to her heart.

'You say you love me too much? Well, let me tell you something: what you're doing isn't borne out of love, it's out-and-out selfishness.'

How could he say that? She tried to tell herself he was just hurt and he was saying these cruel things to hurt her back. She wouldn't have tried to hang on to their friendship if she hadn't loved him. She wouldn't have given up a chance to be with someone she loved more than she'd ever loved before if she wasn't doing it out of love for them. For their own good. Selfish was the exact opposite of what she'd felt.

But his angry words continued. 'If you loved me that much you'd want me to have what I want. But you don't want that.' He took a breath and leaned back from her, his voice dropping an octave. 'You don't love me enough, Maggie; that's the problem here. If you did it would be tangled up with trust, more than a little faith in the kind of man I am and a really strong belief in my ability to love you. This isn't about you doing the best thing for me. It's about you being too scared to try.'

She blinked at him as the tears washed down her cheeks, in rivers this time. Because he might just be right. She might have made the biggest mistake of her life.

Sean stepped back from her, ran a frustrated hand through his dark hair again. Then looked away from her, as if he couldn't stand the sight of her.

'Just remember this was your choice, not mine.' He started to walk away. 'How I feel obviously doesn't matter a damn.'

CHAPTER SIXTEEN

SHE wasn't prepared to go on camera the next day.
But she needed to be in control of one part of her
life when she'd made the rest of it such an unholy
mess.

Still, as she glanced at her reflection in the rear-
view mirror she knew she wasn't exactly going to
portray a professional image. A night spent alter-
nately crying and staring into the darkness while
wind buffeted against the thick walls of the house
had done nothing for her camera face. But this story
called for her to be there. She had to be there. Even
though the long night-time hours had brought her to
several newsflashes of her own.

Like the fact that the reasoning that had brought
her along her Sean-less path in the first place might
have been completely and utterly wrong.

Selfish, he had called her. And she had spent the
long hours after he'd left her both hating him and
crying because of it. Because she really hadn't been
aiming for selfish, she'd been aiming to do what she
honestly believed to be the only honourable thing.

When a person loved someone as much as she
loved Sean they wanted only the good things for
them. Especially when they'd already obviously been
through so much. It had been what she thought was

a completely selfless, if heartbreaking decision. It had also been wrong.

As someone who was trained to listen to what people had to say, not to prejudge or go into any given situation with her heart leading her and not her mind, she should really have known better. But with her heart more than a little involved it had been tougher to stand back and look at the overall picture. And that lack of judgement had led her to doing the one thing she would never have intentionally done. Which was hurt Sean. Deeply.

She was an idiot.

That conclusion then led her to another: how on earth did she deserve him now? After she'd been so very stupid, how could he even still want her?

Then, somewhere between darkness and the first long tendrils of light that dawn brought through her curtains, she felt a glimmer of hope.

He loved her.

He loved her even though she'd been a complete idiot and tried to push him away.

He loved her even though she'd blatantly tried to find someone else right underneath his nose.

He loved her even though she might not be able to give him the one thing she so dearly wanted to be able to give him.

Sean was a strong, caring man. Her friend. And he was fighting to keep her. How could she not fight equally as hard for something so precious, so rare?

Even she couldn't be *that* stupid.

He wasn't going to make it easy for her, though.

By the time she got the call to go to work he'd already left. So she had to make the drive to the coast alone, rehearsing over and over in her mind what she was going to say to him.

I've been a complete idiot, would certainly be a place to start.

With her car parked, she zipped up her waterproof jacket, bowed her head against the rain and went in search of him. She found him wandering around, camera on shoulder, focusing from face to face in the crowd.

She took a deep breath, forced her emotions down and walked to his side. 'Anything yet?'

He lowered his camera and glanced at her from the corner of his eye. 'No, they're still looking.'

Maggie nodded and glanced round, taking in the worried faces that surrounded them. She recognised a few of the businessmen they had interviewed, nodded in response to a couple. She'd never expected to be back here so soon, or for this reason—a fishing boat was missing out at sea.

'How many on board?'

'Six.' He swung the camera down to his side, studying her face with his dark eyes. He noted how she took in the scene with professional eyes, before looking up at him. But the flush that appeared on her cheeks surprised him, and he frowned. 'What?'

She looked down at his large feet rather than continuing looking into his perceptive eyes. Suddenly as shy as a young girl with a crush, she blurted, 'Sean, I've been a complete idiot and—'

'I'm well aware of how stupid you've been, but this isn't the time or the place.'

'I just need to…' She stepped towards him as he swung his camera up and stepped away from her.

His face was emotionless as he looked at her. 'You should know—the boat is the one we were on before. We know these guys.'

Her green eyes widened as she searched his eyes for confirmation of the words. And there it was. The silent sincerity she knew so well. 'Mike McCabe's boat?'

He nodded. 'Yes.'

The dull tone that indicated at the brutal truth made her take a step back. Suddenly their problems had to take a back seat. She could see the faces of the crew she'd interviewed as clearly as if they were right in front of her, could hear their voices and see them at work. She thought about that day on the water, how ill she'd been with a small amount of wind. What must it be like for them now, out there in gale-force winds, stuck on the water without a way home? And she knew without even taking time to think that telling their story, whether the outcome was good or bad, was way more important.

She just hoped that the reactions she'd got from Sean so far were due to the situation the crew were facing rather than his not wanting to hear how wrong she'd been.

Sean could read her face. He reached for her arm, squeezed, and kept his voice calm. 'We have to go do this. Anything else will have to wait.' He stepped closer. 'Take a breath, Maggie, and focus.' He jerked his head towards the small crowd. 'Then go talk to those people, let them see you care, and we'll make sure that everyone understands what they're going through. Listen to them the way I know you can.'

Some of his reliable strength seeped through her jacket and into her veins. She drew from it, let it make its way to her spine so that she straightened a barely perceptible inch and her inner fear was temporarily removed as she lifted her hand and wrapped her fingers around his. She even managed a small smile as she squeezed. 'Let's go.'

He released her hand, turned and pointed towards a hall. 'That's the community centre over there. Most of the families are in there.'

'Then that's where we go.'

Having already spent time in the village stood them in good stead, as did the fact that nearly everyone knew Maggie's face. They found her easy to talk to; she was one of them, a friend who visited their living rooms for a few minutes every evening at six. So they opened up, talked about how many times there had been storms and they'd lain awake at night praying that all the boats would come home. Told tales from generations ago of fathers and grandfathers who hadn't come home or had come home without friends.

It was powerful stuff and Maggie felt their fear as clearly as if it were her own.

She stayed with Jean McCabe and her daughters-in-law even when the camera stopped rolling. Sean stayed for a while too,‾ teasing stories from them about the men that were missing, taking their minds off the waiting for a short while. He smiled, charmed smiles from them in return, and Maggie realised how easily the women opened up to him. She knew what it was like to feel comfort in his quiet strength, to warm to his laughter and forget the outside world for brief moments. It was just something in him, an intangible part of his character. Yet another of the many reasons she loved him and should have believed in him.

After a while he glanced her way, the spark in his eyes fading. And then he simply stood up and, as Maggie continued talking to the other women, he disappeared.

After a while she missed the sight of his tall frame, sought him out with her eyes. Maybe it was a kind of reassurance to her to be able to look at him when she was surrounded by so many people who couldn't look at the men they loved.

The thought of what she still had to say to him was like a dull, throbbing headache at the back of her skull, the lack of light in his eyes when he'd looked at her causing her to fear once again that she'd done too much damage.

But even though she turned all the way round in her chair she still couldn't see him.

There was a flurry at the doorway as someone pushed in and she realised above the hum of voices that the wind had picked up again. It had been a long time since the autumn had been heralded by such fierce winds.

Standing up, she looked around again. *Where was he?* Her eyes scanned the long table where comforting mugs of sweetened tea were being handed out. It was what all Irish people did in a crisis—drank tea and told funny stories to keep the demons at bay. But Sean wasn't drinking tea.

Frowning, she looked down at the seat where he'd been, her eyes searching for his camera. It wasn't there. Was there something going on outside?

She lifted her jacket from the back of her own chair and made her excuses, squeezing Mike's wife's hand as she told her she'd be 'right back'. Then she walked to the door, yanked it open and went in search of Sean.

The rain was coming sideways at her as she walked towards the stone jetty where policemen and an ambulance were waiting. One of the rescue boats had come back and while she pulled her hood up over her head she saw the familiar orange of Sean's jacket. As she got closer she realised he was pulling a life-jacket on over it.

'What are you doing?' She had to shout to make her voice heard over the wind.

Turning his head, he watched her approach, waited until she was close enough for him not to have to shout the words. 'I'm going out with the crew.'

Her eyes widened, she looked out at the huge waves beyond the harbour and then back up into his dark eyes. 'In that? No, you're not!'

'Yes, I am. I cleared it with Joe.'

'It's too dangerous for us to be out there!' Her anger rose at his having talked to Joe without talking to her first. They always worked as a team, and even though Sean's experience of crisis situations went well beyond hers she was hurt that he hadn't talked to her. It was yet another echo of the problems they were having.

'*We're* not going. I am.' He lugged his camera up from the ground and started along the jetty.

Her heart went crazy, her feet immediately following him. 'You can't go out there, Sean.'

'It's what we do, remember? All I'm going to do is film the rescue crew while they look for *The Sally*.'

'Then I'm coming too.'

'No, you're not.'

She had to run a couple of steps to catch him, her hand on his arm as she spun round to face him. 'We're a team, where you go, I go.'

'Oh, is that the way it works?'

Her breath caught. 'You can't do this because you're mad at me!'

Sean laughed. 'You think that's why I'm doing this? I'm not doing this because I'm mad at you, Maggie, I'm doing it because it's our job.'

'*Our* job.'

'Yes, *our* job.' He set his camera against his hip, turned his arm from her grasp and then lifted it to set his large hand on her shoulder. He leaned closer, his voice just loud enough for her to hear. 'And I'm going 'cos this is the stuff we get paid to do. But you can't swim, Maggie, so there's no way in hell I'm letting you go out there. It's *my* job to look out for *you*.'

And he always had. They were a team, a partnership. That was what they each did for the other. Or at least it had been. Before she'd messed it up.

Looking into his eyes close up, she knew there was just no way she was going to stop him. She watched as he looked back at her, saw something shimmer across the dark depths so familiar to her, felt the hesitation. Then he squeezed her shoulder and lugged his camera up again.

'Be careful.'

His smile was slow. 'I always am.'

'No, I mean more careful than that.'

He stood for a moment longer. Then he simply turned and walked to the bright red boat.

Her feet carried her forward as he stepped off the jetty and her voice rose above the wind. 'I love you.'

His head dropped, then rose as he turned to look back at her, his fringe whipping into his eyes. 'I know,' he yelled back, 'you told me.'

'I didn't tell you the right way.' Her voice wobbled as she continued to shout across at him.

Sean studied her as the boat's crew moved around him, then he shrugged, his face still deadpan. 'Tell me later.'

The boat pulled out and Maggie watched until she couldn't read the word 'Rescue' on the side any more.

It took half an hour and rain dripping off the end

of her nose before she went back into the hall. Standing on the dock without him had brought a sense of loneliness as she'd never had before. And with that sense of loneliness came the need for the company of other women who understood what it was like.

Grabbing a huge mug of sweetened tea from the table, she went back and listened as they talked. They chatted about their kids, what was on offer at the supermarket, who had been on holiday to where. Normal conversation. But with a look in their eyes that told Maggie their thoughts weren't on the conversation.

'Where's that good-looking camera guy, then?'

She looked Mike's wife in the eye. 'He went out on the rescue boat.'

'In this storm? Is his head cut?'

The old phrase made her smile. 'Sometimes I wonder.'

The older woman seemed to recognise something in her voice. She leaned out and squeezed Maggie's hand in her lap. 'He'll be grand. They know what they're doing, those boys.'

'How do you do it?' The question broke free from her mouth. 'I mean, watch the people you care about go out there in this kind of weather?'

There was a shrug of shoulders as she leaned back in her chair. 'They do what they have to do. Everybody has families to support and bills to pay. It just happens to be their job to go out in all weathers.'

Maggie nodded at the answer.

Her eyes seemed to consider Maggie's for a long moment, then she leaned forward in her seat. 'Maybe I'm just more used with it now. I never used to sleep at the start. That first year we were married, when the storms came, I didn't sleep till he was home.'

'You worried you'd lose him.' Maggie understood how that felt and had an instant affinity with her because of it. She, too, leaned forward, until their heads almost touched, her voice low. 'You must have wondered sometimes if it mightn't have been easier to fall for someone who worked indoors.'

She laughed and shook her head. 'Aye. But you don't get to pick who you fall for. You just be thankful you found it and you hold on for grim death while you have it. God forbid that he didn't come back but if it ever happened I still wouldn't swap a minute.'

'You love him very much.'

'That I do.' Her eyes shone before she looked down at her lap. 'He's my best friend, Mike is; been there for all the hard times and we wouldn't be without each other. We're very blessed.'

'Yes.' Maggie reached forward and returned the reassuring squeeze of hands. 'He'll be here in no time.'

She nodded. Then she raised her eyes in question. 'You got a thing goin' on with that camera guy of yours?'

It was an almost automatic reaction to immediately deny it. But Maggie's heart was too clearly on her sleeve for her to do that, especially after the trust that had just been shown her. The thought of Sean so far away from her while things were still so strained tore her up. To even think for a second that something might happen to him out there in her own personal nightmare land…

She wasn't going to do it. She wasn't going to fear the worst and worry. Instead it appeared she was going to sit and pour out her heart to a virtual stranger in a tiny country community hall. Over sweetened tea.

It was a kind of rehearsal, that was all. A 'coming out' of sorts. She would shout it to the world if that was what it took to show Sean that she was his.

She started with a nod. 'It's complicated, though.'

'Ah, sure it always is. Are you in love?'

'Yes.'

'He in love with you, is he?'

'Yes.' If she hadn't managed to kill the emotion in him. Not that she really deserved his love after all she'd done to them both.

There was an answering nod. 'You'd think it wouldn't be that complicated, then.'

Maggie smiled. 'You'd think.'

'Who made it complicated?'

She felt herself grimace inside. 'That would be me.'

Another nod. 'Women do that more than men. They don't think things inside out like we do.'

'Oh, no, Sean thinks.' She laughed affectionately. 'He thinks more clearly than I do sometimes.'

'Because you try to think too much?'

'Yes, I think so.' She smiled at what she'd just said. 'See what I mean?'

The door opened and everyone's eyes were immediately drawn towards the people coming in. But they saw when their hoods came down that it was just more of the local wives appearing with trays of food.

Maggie leaned back a little but Mike's wife stayed close. 'Would you be without him?'

'I tried—it wasn't nice. And I think I really hurt him doing it.'

'There you go thinking again. You should try just doin' some feelin'.' Her eyes strayed to the door, then back into Maggie's eyes as she took a breath. 'Y'know, sometimes I'm awful glad to see Mike go out on that boat. But I still love it when he comes back. I might hate him from time to time, get angry at him, need time away from him, but he's still my man. I wouldn't be without him.'

Any more than Maggie would be without Sean. She was glad it wouldn't take a tragedy of some kind for her to understand that. All it had taken was for him to tell her she'd been a selfish idiot, and there weren't too many people who loved her enough to say that to her face.

The thing was, throughout all of her great scheme she had never wanted him to be out of her life completely. Because if she had she would have just let him go. She would have moved away from him, changed her job, shut him out of her life. But she hadn't been able to do that completely, had she?

She'd tried hard to hang on. And in doing so he'd eventually found his way to the truth.

Maybe because, deep down, she had *wanted* him to?

While she blinked at the wise woman in front of her, the truth slowly started to appear. What Sean had said to her about being selfish *was* true. She might have persuaded herself she was trying to be selfless and self-sacrificing for the man she loved, but what if the simple truth was she had needed him to *prove* she wasn't wrong about him? Had she needed him to be strong, to fight to keep her, to show her he loved her by pushing and pushing to get her to lean on him, to trust in him? So that she would know he would never leave her when things got bad? The way Tony had with her sister?

Had she been *testing* him?

The realisation certainly made her *feel* selfish. Who was she to do that to him? Who was she to test the strength of a man who had almost destroyed his soul showing people the kind of cruelty and injustice that could exist in the world? How could she do that to someone she loved so much?

It had taken Jean McCabe, a stranger, a woman who was the facing the very real possibility of losing the man who meant as much to her as Sean did to Maggie, to open her eyes a little wider than even her sleepless night had managed.

Without thinking about it Maggie leaned forward and enfolded Mike's wife in her arms. She turned her head to speak into her ear. 'Have a little faith, Jean.'

As they pulled apart she smiled into Maggie's face with shimmering eyes. 'Aye, I will. You too.'

Suddenly desperate to see Sean again, she walked outside and back to the jetty. Boats were still moored there, their sides being thrust back and forth against the buoys tied to rings embedded in the stone.

And it was there she stood for a long, long while. Thinking about what she could say to right such a wrong. She rehearsed different versions of 'sorry' over and over again. Until the light began to dim and it was almost dark, the rain falling in silver streaks through the emergency lights. For the first time she shuddered beneath her jacket as a sliver of fear crossed her chest.

'Where are you?'

Suddenly, far into the black waves, she could see lights. And then there was a call. 'It's them! It just came over the radio from the coastguard—they've got them!'

Her legs carried her to the man's side. 'Are they all OK?'

'Yes, they found *The Sally* about a mile off shore; she was pretty beat up, had a fire on board so no radio. She was taking on water; one of the crew has a broken arm. But they're fine. Rescue boat had a time of it getting her secured to the tug, though.'

She felt her stomach threaten to release the tea she'd drunk, 'What happened?'

'It banged its hull pretty bad off *The Sally* in them

waves but they're all OK. Everyone's coming back in now.'

She could have hugged him. Instead she yelled a 'Thanks' and ran into the hall so that everyone could be there to see the boats come in.

They stood there, the families of the crew, hand in hand on the stone jetty as one by one the boats started to reappear. Then they saw the tugboat towing *The Sally* and a cheer went up.

Maggie let the bodies push past her while she searched for a familiar orange jacket on a rescue boat. As one of the spotlights was swung towards *The Sally* she finally saw it, running slightly in front. And there he was, standing on the narrow deck, his camera trained first upwards onto the trawler-boat crew and then sweeping across the harbour to the faces of the people who waited. Doing his job. Getting on with it without fuss or complaint. Just with that silent strength of his, the strength that she should have believed in.

While the boat got closer he set the camera down, waved at the crew of *The Sally* and then looked back at the jetty. His head turned as he searched across its length. And stopped when he found Maggie. But he didn't raise a hand to wave, didn't smile. He just nodded, and turned away.

Maggie's heart sank. What if he couldn't trust in her any more? What if he was so disappointed in her that he couldn't ever look at her again? What if she really had killed some of the love he had for her?

She was going to take her chances. Because she was his, pure and simple. He would have to see that her idiocy was just a part of the overall package that was Mary Margaret Sullivan.

CHAPTER SEVENTEEN

IT WAS the first time in her life that Maggie had ever known inside that what she said in the next few minutes would have the most profound effect on her world, her state of mind, the condition of her heart for the rest of her days. It was a life-changing kind of a moment.

When Sean insisted that they finish the job in hand before she could try talking to him it had made her heart sink again. Another sign that he had already backed away, his disappointment in her too much to overcome? Or simply that he was still in professional working mode, clearing away the business end of things and giving them time to talk properly? She just didn't know.

Having it pushed back so calmly made her mad though. Now that she had thought everything out with a tad more introspective honesty, she deeply needed to let it all out into the open. And in her frustration she almost said it all on camera.

But to do that in front of the world, to take away some of the inherent intimacy of what she had to say with some kind of a public monologue, would just have been a wrong on top of a wrong on top of a wrong.

However, waiting was killing her.

Her green eyes watched nervously from the side as he wandered around, his head bowed, camera swinging from one large hand. He raised his head, the wind catching his dark hair and whisking his fringe into his eyes as it had when he'd stood on the rescue boat and told her he knew she loved him. He didn't really though, did he? Because she'd been fooling herself about how she really felt and what she'd said hadn't been completely the truth. So he couldn't know.

Reaching up, he brushed the hair back with long fingers as his eyes sought hers. Deep dark brown met with green and where a smile had once automatically appeared his mouth remained still.

Maggie couldn't see the look in his eyes but her memory served her well enough from the night before.

She knew if she looked she would see a glint of the pain he tried so hard to hide. She would see the disappointment he had in her. And it was like being punched in the chest knowing those things were there.

Her palms went damp, clammy. With a shaky breath she watched him until he frowned and looked away from her. Then she wiped her hands along the edges of her jeans and tried to go over the words she'd rehearsed.

There was movement from their left and another camera crew gravitated towards the hall door. Maggie felt her feet pulled in that direction, she felt her heart thump in her chest. This was it. It was time for the interviews.

After the interviews she would stand in front of the camera and give her closing report.

And then, the most important set of words of her life.

Sean still barely managed to look at her even while he filmed. He followed the families as they were reunited, wandered amongst the crowd, catching comments and facial expressions. He filmed Maggie interviewing the rescue crews. Basically he'd been a pro every step of the way—calm, assured, focused on the task in front of him. Detached.

He knew that was what he did when things got close to his emotions. He shut them out. Did what he had to do. But even when he stopped Maggie from trying to talk over the previous night he was feeling his heart struggle to break free from that detachment. To make him feel the inner anguish at having messed up so badly with her when he'd lost his temper and said she was selfish.

Yes, he was angry that she didn't have more faith in him. Yes, he was mad that she was prepared to throw away something that had become so incredibly precious to him without talking it through first. Yes, he was frustrated that he'd been forced to such devious levels to try and get her to see that he was right for her, only to have her use the very emotion he wanted from her to push him away.

But none of that was reason enough for him to have lost his temper with her when she was already tortured enough. He should have been more patient. Should have taken the time to understand her reasoning and debate where she'd got it wrong. Calmly. In a reassuring manner. Letting her know he wasn't going anywhere.

Instead he now had her pussy-footing around him, looking so nervous that the drop of a pin would have made her jump a mile. She was trying to find a kinder way to let him down easy, wasn't she?

Oh, yeah, he'd messed this up big time.

'Maggie?' His voice sounded in front of her. 'Hey, Maggie.'

Her eyes shot towards his and were met with a quirked eyebrow. She blinked and answered with a slightly breathless, 'Yes?'

He frowned, then jerked his head in the direction of the people in front of them. 'Interview?'

'Yeah, I got it.' She waited until he turned away, shook her head and walked forward. Just this and the round-up and then it was time. She could do this.

And she did, ending the interviews with her jaw aching from smiling a forced smile for the camera. Which brought her one step closer to confession time.

Ten minutes later he set his camera down off his shoulder and glared at her. 'OK, that's it. Did you schedule a lobotomy that I missed?'

Maggie blinked at him. 'What?'

'Let's just say that your round-up is a little sideways. Maybe you should just tell me what's going on and get it over and done with.'

On the round-up he did have point. Three takes because she couldn't say the word 'tempestuous'. But, in fairness, there had been other times. Like the time the Russian dancers had been touring and she hadn't been even within hitting distance of pronouncing their names right without them all dissolving into fits of giggles. That time, though, she hadn't had an excuse as good as this one.

'I'll get it.' She waved her hand at him to get him to lift the camera. 'Let's go.'

'Not till you tell me what's going on.' He tilted his head and stared at her.

'Right now, this minute?'

'Right now, this minute.'

Maggie stared at him.

'Well?' Sean kept his head tilted to one side so he could look at her outside the lens of the camera. He was tired, drained emotionally and physically with the events of the day, the night before, and the ones he knew were headed his way. 'Spit it out, Maggie, so we can get finished up and get out of here.'

She stared at him some more, then took a breath. 'I kind of had a planned speech. And you're ruining it.'

His patience was running out. 'Damn it, whatever the hell it is, just spill it and let's do this.'

'OK, fine.' Her hands rose to plant themselves on her hips. 'I just wanted to let you know you were right and I was wrong and I'm in love with you and I don't want to lose you and I've been an idiot. That's all.'

Funny, it didn't seem so bad when it was spoken so quickly. She frowned at him, her voice calmer. 'But for the record, I had planned to say it better than that.'

Dark eyes stared at her, long, dark lashes blinking slowly. 'Well, maybe you should try it the way you planned.'

Pursing her lips, she looked away from him, her arms moving again to cross over her breasts. 'No, you've ruined it now.'

'I might take more convincing.'

The old saying of hate being the flip side of love was on the mark. Much as she knew she had to fight, had to work harder to get him to believe her, her pride still hated the fact that she'd been so very wrong in the first place, that pride forcing her shoulders up a barely perceptible inch.

But Sean saw it, saw it and almost laughed aloud with relief. She wasn't trying to let him down easy. 'Go on, I'm listening.'

She scowled at him from the corner of her eye. 'I hate you for going out on that boat by the way, it really sucked. You shouldn't have gone out there without me!'

'I'm sorry, is that what you rehearsed? Being mad at me? That's gonna win me over all right.'

Her voice rose. 'What if your boat had hit the other boat harder? What if you'd fallen in the water and that bloody camera had dragged you under? 'Cos I know you wouldn't have let go of the damned thing! How do you think that would have felt to me?'

His mouth quirked at her reasoning. 'That's a bit melodramatic, don't you think? And anyway, you'd already decided to let me go, so what would it have mattered?'

'It would have mattered.' Her voice dropped an octave. 'It would have mattered because I'd never have had a chance to let you know I believe in you. I *do*.' She waggled a finger in his direction. 'And I may be being melodramatic about the dumb boat but if you'd just let me tell you all this stuff earlier then I wouldn't have spent hours feeling this frustrated.'

'Why?'

She blinked in confusion. 'What?'

'Why do you believe in me now? Why not months ago when you found out you had to fight for that family you want? Why not last night when I told you how I felt?'

For a woman who spent most of her life using words to paint a picture she suddenly found them hard to find. Her feet carried her forward, encouraged by the fact he stood his ground. Then, inches from him, she turned her eyes up to his and took a breath. 'I think too much, Sean.' She smiled sadly. 'You know that about me. And you were right, I was being selfish, no matter what I might have told myself to justify it.'

He stayed absolutely still. 'Go on.'

She took another breath. 'Sometimes you can just want something too much. I wanted everything to be so right—a great guy, amazing kids, a dog, bloody roses round the door. I found the great guy, and I think I loved him for a long time before I knew it. I was almost ready to tell him, because I could, I don't know,' she shrugged, 'almost *feel* that he felt the same way. But then I found out that the amazing kids weren't going to be an option for me. Not without risking the heartbreak that my sister went through. And I didn't want that for me and this great guy.'

'Life isn't perfect.'

'No, it isn't. But I watched what they went through, from the sidelines, and I felt her pain every time there wasn't a baby. I know I'd hurt that much, and I know that you'd hurt because I hurt.'

His jaw clenched and unclenched.

'I told myself that it wasn't fair to do that to you when you'd already hurt so much.' Her voice wobbled and she had to take a moment to clear her throat. 'I told myself that I had to let you go because you deserve to be happy after all you've been through.'

When she paused and continued to stare at him he almost relented. But he knew he was safe now, and he knew she needed to get months of hurt out, so he stood his ground, kept his voice calm. 'That wasn't your choice to make alone.'

'I know that now.' Her throat was closing over at the sight of him remaining so calm and detached. She really had ruined this, hadn't she? 'I should have trusted you and I should have talked to you.'

'Why didn't you?'

Her voice finally cracked, tears welling in her eyes as she turned her head and tried to blink them away.

'Because I was just too scared to lose you. I thought giving you up would be easier.'

There was a moment's silence and then his deep voice sounded close to her ear. 'For someone so incredibly smart you really can be very dumb.'

When she looked round with shimmering eyes, his face was right by hers. 'I know,' she swallowed and tried a small smile, 'but the truth is I'm not brave enough to lose you.'

Searching her eyes for long moments, he then allowed himself to look from the hair on her forehead, down over her arched brows, her tear-filled eyes, her fine nose, her full mouth, to the stubborn chin she normally held so high. And he'd never loved her more.

'You were never going to lose me. Just get that straight for starters.'

Two large, fat tears escaped from the edges of her eyes. 'I never wanted to, not really.'

'I know.'

She watched as he set the camera down at his feet, his head bowing for a brief second. Then, as her eyes met his again, she watched in wonder as he smiled softly and raised his large hands to frame her face.

'You done?'

She shook her head.

'Hurry up, then.'

A small cough cleared her throat. 'I really need you to know that I do believe in you, more than I could ever tell you. But I also need to tell you that...'

and then her voice broke and she had to choke out the words '...I want a baby with you, Sean.'

His voice was as choked as hers. 'I want that, too.'

'But I might not be able to do that.'

'I know.' His thumbs moved back and forth against her cheeks, moving the tears as they fell. He leaned his forehead down to touch hers. 'You finished now?'

All she could manage was a nod.

'OK, then, my turn.' He ducked down an inch or two to meet her eyes up close. 'I was never going to let you run off with a Bryan or a Paul. Because you're mine. It's just that simple.'

A soft sob broke free.

'We're going to do this together, no matter how hard it gets. And if it doesn't happen then it'll be OK, because we'll still have each other.'

And another sob, from deeper in her soul this time.

'There are hundreds of kids out there who need two parents to love them. You don't have to have a family the old-fashioned way for it to be a family.'

She'd never loved him more.

'So here's how it's gonna be.'

She listened.

'You and I are going to get married. We're going to find a house, we can plant bloody roses round the door if you want, and I'm all for a dog.'

She laughed.

Sean smiled a lop-sided smile at her, his eyes sparkling. 'We're gonna go find out about all our options when it comes to having a baby and we're gonna try our damnedest to make it happen.'

She leaned forward and kissed him hard.

'Wait, I haven't finished.' He dropped his hands to her shoulders and held her back. 'We're gonna find kids who need us and we're gonna spend the rest of our lives being happy and working damn hard at staying that way.'

She nodded and tried to lean forward again.

But he ducked his head out of the way. 'Still not finished over here.' A dark brow rose in warning. 'You are never, ever gonna try holding something back from me again, because I warn you, I'll find out.'

There was another attempt for a kiss.

'Would you quit it?' He laughed, despite his stern tone. 'I haven't even got to the serious stuff.'

'You've said enough. I love you.'

His inner joy broke free in an almost arrogant raise of his chin and a confidently spoken, 'Course you do.' He then used his hands on her shoulders to rock her from side to side. 'And I love you. But the thing I need you to remember, Mary Margaret, is, I *need* you.' He stopped the rocking, his voice husky. 'Being your friend brought me out of the dark and I don't know that I could have done that without you.'

'Yes, you could.'

He shook his head. 'I don't think so. You taught me how to feel something real and precious. That's a miracle in itself.'

And it was. There was no arguing that. Maggie

had fought against the one thing that made any sense, the one thing that so few people found in the world. She wasn't going to fight it any more. And in her heart she honestly believed that if they'd found one miracle then someone, somewhere was looking out for them. So maybe other miracles were possible too, like that family she'd always wanted. It was just a case of believing.

'You done now?'

He made an exaggerated nod. 'Yep.'

'So, can I kiss you properly now?'

'Any time you want.' Lifting his hands from her shoulders, he held his arms out at his sides in surrender. 'I'm all yours.'

Maggie smiled up at his ridiculous lop-sided grin. She stepped forward so that her body touched all along the length of his, wrapped her arms around his neck, tangled her fingers in his hair and drew his mouth down to hers. 'And I'm all yours. I always was.'

EPILOGUE

'I'M GLAD u're happy Mary.'

She smiled down at the screen when the words appeared. She almost felt guilty for having to let go of her new 'friend'. But she had found him at a time she had needed to, had talked to him when she hadn't been able to talk to Sean. He had helped her through. So she owed him a goodbye and an explanation for the goodbye.

'It'll happen for you, you wait and see.'

The musical note came back quickly. *'U never know.'*

He was too nice a guy for it not to happen. But she knew there weren't always miracles for everyone. The thought made her sad. Everyone should have the bond she had with Sean.

'Have faith.'

'I'll do my best.' There was a pause for several minutes and then, *'Did u wonder how he found out?'*

Her brows creased down slightly. She had. It hadn't occurred to her at the time and when it had she had thought that Kath must have told him. Something she could have forgiven her for, considering the outcome. But in her heart she knew that Kath wouldn't have done that, no matter how wrong Maggie had been at the time. They were sisters, and that was what sisters did. They trusted each other, made promises that wouldn't be broken.

So she'd had to put it down to Sean knowing her better than she'd realised. He'd been right about so many things and, knowing Kath's history as well as he did, he must just have figured it out. It didn't really matter now.

'I did, but it doesn't really make a difference. Things turn out the way they're supposed to, and I'm learning not to over-think any more.'

'Wow, r u sure u're a girl?'

Maggie laughed. *'Quite sure.'*

'Well, I'm impressed. He must b a great guy.'

That didn't take too much thinking about. *'He is. You'd like him. You have a similar sense of humour.'*

'Sarcastic at inappropriate times?'

Maggie laughed. *'Yep.'*

'Maybe in another life we might have been made 4 each other, u and me.'

'In another life, maybe.'

She glanced at the clock on the bottom of her screen, then moved her fingers across the keyboard. *'I have to go. You keep the faith, you hear?'*

'Believe in the miracle?'

Her eyes blinked at the words. *'Yes.'*

'Good luck, Mary.'

'Thanks for being a friend, Romeo.'

There was a pause again and then the note sounded for the last time. *'Always.'*

She stared at the screen long after he'd signed off, a niggling voice in the back of her head from the echoes she'd felt in his words. Then she laughed and shut the computer down. There she was, over-thinking again. It was ridiculous. But hey, maybe in another life Romeo would have been her Sean.

Her heart beat a little faster as she checked her appearance in the mirror, grabbed her wrap and pulled open her front door.

The door facing hers opened at the same time and they grinned at each other across the hallway.

'I was wondering…'

'Wondering what?' She pulled her door closed behind her and stepped towards him.

A spark of familiar devilment entered his dark eyes. Pulling his own door closed, he leaned back against it and watched her approach. 'I was wondering if you'd mind terribly if I held your hand?'

She smiled and held out her hand, palm upwards. 'That would be OK.'

'And I was wondering—' he placed his larger hand on hers and wrapped his fingers around hers '—if it would be an awful inconvenience to ask for a kiss?'

Maggie laughed. 'Ha, ha.'

He leaned in and kissed her, slowly, deliberately, until Maggie's knees turned to mush.

'And I was curious to know,' the words were whispered against her swollen mouth, 'if you'd maybe like to…'

Maggie listened as he leaned close to her ear to whisper his question. She blushed a fiery red and felt the heat radiate all over her body.

Sean leaned his head back and looked down into her eyes. He smiled his lop-sided smile as he asked, 'Well?'

'Well...' she wrapped her arms around his neck '...I did have a hot date lined up, but seeing as you asked so nicely...'

His mouth stayed attached to hers as he opened the door to his apartment and backed them inside. 'Maybe we should go see about that honeymoon suite of ours at some point, too. We could put it to better use this time...'

There was still the matter of a few confessions he had to make to her as well. Confessions of underhandedness and his devious nature. But he reckoned if he was going to confess one last little secret, then he needed to butter Maggie up a little first. The way he figured it, another twenty-four hours might just do the trick.

After all, she'd gone looking on that site of hers for the perfect guy. The way Sean saw it, she'd found him.

Someone just like him.

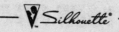
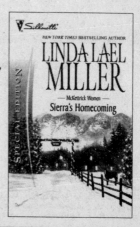

REQUEST YOUR FREE BOOKS!

2 FREE NOVELS PLUS 2 FREE GIFTS!

SILHOUETTE
Romance®

From Today to Forever...

SROM06

SILHOUETTE *Romance*®

COMING NEXT MONTH

#1838 PLAIN JANE'S PRINCE CHARMING—Melissa McClone
When waitress Jane Dawson approaches millionaire Chase Ryder to
sponsor her charity, she is thrilled when he agrees. Deep down she
knows there is no chance sexy Chase will be interested in a plain
Jane like her! But Jane's passion to help others is a breath of fresh
air to Chase, and he soon realizes that Jane is a woman in a million,
and deserves her very own happy ending.

#1839 THE TYCOON'S INSTANT FAMILY—
Caroline Anderson
When handsome business tycoon Nick Barron hires
Georgie Cauldwell to help with his property development, they
spend a few gorgeously romantic weeks together. Then Nick
disappears! When he returns, it is with two young children and a
tiny baby. Georgie knows she shouldn't fall in love with a man
who has a family, but there is something about this family she
can't resist.

#1840 HAVING THE BOSS'S BABIES—Barbara Hannay
Like the rest of the staff at Kanga Tours, Alice Madigan is nervous
about meeting her new boss. But when he walks through the door
it's worse than she could ever have imagined! She shared one
very special night with him—and now they have to play it strictly
business! But for how long can they pretend nothing happened?

#1841 HOW TO MARRY A BILLIONAIRE—Ally Blake
Cara Marlowe's new TV job will make her career—as long
as nothing goes wrong. So it's bad news when billionaire
Adam Tyler wants the show stopped, and worse that Cara
can hardly concentrate with the gorgeous tycoon around! Cara
wants Adam—and her job, too. Will she have to make a choice?

SRCNM1006